Also by Andrea Camilleri

Hunting Season

To request Penguin Readers Guides by mail
(while supplies last), please call (800) 778–6425
or e-mail reading@us.penguingroup.com.
To access Penguin Readers Guide online,
visit our Web site at www.penguin.com.

Elvira Giorgianni

AUGUST HEAT

Andrea Camilleri, a bestseller in Italy and Germany, is the author of the popular and *New York Times* bestselling Inspector Montalbano series, as well as historical novels set in nineteenth-century Sicily. The Montalbano series has been translated into thirty-two languages and was adapted for Italian television. *The Potter's Field*, the thirteenth book in the series, was awarded the Crime Writers' Association's International Dagger for the best crime novel translated into English. He lives in Italy.

AUGUST HEAT

ANDREA CAMILLERI

Translated by Stephen Sartarelli

PENGUIN BOOKS

PENGUIN BOOKS
Published by the Penguin Group
Penguin Group (USA) Inc., 375 Hudson Street, New York, New York 10014, U.S.A.
Penguin Group (Canada), 90 Eglinton Avenue East, Suite 700, Toronto,
Ontario, Canada M4P 2Y3 (a division of Pearson Penguin Canada Inc.)
Penguin Books Ltd, 80 Strand, London WC2R 0RL, England
Penguin Ireland, 25 St Stephen's Green, Dublin 2, Ireland (a division of Penguin Books Ltd)
Penguin Group (Australia), 250 Camberwell Road, Camberwell,
Victoria 3124, Australia (a division of Pearson Australia Group Pty Ltd)
Penguin Books India Pvt Ltd, 11 Community Centre,
Panchsheel Park, New Delhi – 110 017, India
Penguin Group (NZ), 67 Apollo Drive, Rosedale, North Shore 0632,
New Zealand (a division of Pearson New Zealand Ltd)
Penguin Books (South Africa) (Pty) Ltd, 24 Sturdee Avenue,
Rosebank, Johannesburg 2196, South Africa

Penguin Books Ltd, Registered Offices:
80 Strand, London WC2R 0RL, England

First published in Penguin Books 2009

1   3   5   7   9   10   8   6   4   2

Originally published in Italian as *La vampa d'agosto* by Sellerio Editore, Palermo.
Copyright © 2006 Sellerio Editore.

LIBRARY OF CONGRESS CATALOGING IN PUBLICATION DATA
Camilleri, Andrea.
[Vampa d'agosto. English]
August heat / Andrea Camilleri; translated by Stephen Sartarelli.
p. cm.—(A Penguin mystery original)
ISBN 978-0-14-311405-5
I. Sartarelli, Stephen, ———. II. Title.
PQ4863.A3894V3613 2009
853'.914—dc22   2008029438

Printed in the United States of America
Set in Bembo   Designed by Jaye Zimet

AUGUST HEAT

1

He was sleeping so soundly that not even cannon fire could have woken him. Well, maybe not cannon fire, but the ringing of the telephone, yes.

Nowadays, if a man living in a civilized country (ha!) hears cannon blasts in his sleep, he will, of course, mistake them for thunderclaps, gun salutes on the feast day of the local patron saint, or furniture being moved by the slime-buckets living upstairs, and go right on sleeping soundly. But the ringing of the telephone, the triumphal march of the cell phone, or the doorbell, no: Those are all sounds of summons in response to which the civilized man (ha-ha!) has no choice but to surface from the depths of slumber and answer.

And so Montalbano got up out of bed, glanced at the clock, looked over at the window, gathered that it was going to be a very hot day, and went into the dining room, where the telephone was ringing wildly.

"Salvo! Where were you? I've been trying to call for half an hour!"

"I'm sorry, Livia, I was in the shower, I couldn't hear."

First lie of the day.

Why did he say it? Because he was ashamed to tell Livia he was still asleep? Or because he didn't want to embarrass her by telling her she'd woken him up? Who knows?

"Did you go look at the house?"

"Livia! It's barely eight o'clock!"

"I'm sorry. I'm just so impatient to know if it's all right . . ."

The whole business had started about two weeks before, when he'd had to tell Livia that, contrary to plan, he would not be able to leave Vigàta for the first half of August because Mimì Augello had been forced to take his vacation earlier than expected due to complications with his in-laws. But the change had not produced the calamitous results he had feared. Livia was very fond of Beba, Mimì's wife, and of Mimì himself. She had complained a little, of course, but Montalbano thought that would be the end of it. He was wrong. Way off the mark, in fact. The following evening, Livia had called back with a surprise request.

"I'm looking for a house, right away, two bedrooms with living room, by the sea, in your area."

"I don't understand. Why can't we just stay at my place in Marinella?"

"You can be so stupid, Salvo, when you put your mind to it! I meant a house for Laura, her husband, and their little boy."

Laura was Livia's dearest friend, the one to whom she confided her Joyful and not-so-Joyful Mysteries.

"They're coming here?"

"Yes. Do you mind?"

"Not at all. I think Laura and her husband are very nice, you know that. It's just that . . ."

"It's just what?"

Geez, what a pain!

"I was hoping we could finally spend a little more time together, just the two of us, alone—"

"Ha-ha-ha-ha!"

A laugh rather like that of the witch in *Snow White and the Seven Dwarfs*.

"What's so funny?"

"What's so funny is that you know damn well the only one who's going to be alone is me—me and nobody else—while you're spending your days and maybe even your nights at the station working on the murder of the week!"

"Come on, Livia, it's August. With this kind of heat, even the killers wait until autumn down here."

"Is that some kind of joke? Am I supposed to laugh?"

And thus began the long search for a house, with the help—inconclusive—of Catarella.

"Chief, I tink I gotta place like you's lookin for, out by Pezzodipane."

"But Pezzodipane's six miles from the sea!"

"Iss true, but to make up for it, there's a artifishy lake."

Or:

"Livia, I found a lovely little apartment in a sort of condo near—"

"A *little* apartment? I think I told you clearly, I want a house."

"Well, an apartment's a house, isn't it? What is it, a tent?"

"No, an apartment is not a house. It's you Sicilians who confuse the matter by calling an apartment a house, whereas when I say house, I mean house. You want me to be more specific? I want you to find a freestanding, single-family residence."

The real estate agents in Vigàta laughed in his face.

"What, you think you can come in here on the sixteenth of July and find a house by the sea for the first of August? It was all rented out a long time ago!"

But they'd told him to leave his telephone number. If, by chance, somebody canceled at the last minute, they would let him know. And a miracle did happen, at the very moment he had given up hope.

"Hello, Inspector Montalbano? This is Aurora Real Estate. A nice little villa by the sea has been freed up, the sort of thing you were looking for. It's at Marina di Montereale, in the Pizzo district. But you'd better come by in a hurry, because we're about to close."

He'd run out right in the middle of an interrogation and rushed to the agency. From the photos it looked exactly like what Livia wanted. So he'd arranged with Mr. Callara, the head of the agency, to come pick him up the following morning around nine o'clock to show the house, which was up by Montereale, less than six miles from Marinella.

Montalbano realized that six miles, on the road to Montereale, at the height of summer, could just as easily mean a five-minute drive as a two-hour drive, depending on traffic. Too bad. Livia and Laura would have to make do. It couldn't be helped.

The following morning, as soon as he got in the car, Callara started talking and never stopped. He began with recent history, recounting how the house had been rented to a certain Jacolino, who was a clerk in Cremona and had made the required down payment. But just last night, this Jacolino had phoned the agency saying his wife's mother had just had an accident, and so they couldn't leave Cremona for the time being. And so the agency had called him, Montalbano, right away.

Next, Signor Callara delved into past history. That is, he told him, in full detail, how and why the house had been built. Some six years back, an old fellow of about seventy, who went by the name of Angelo Speciale—Monterealese by birth, but an emigrant to Germany, where he'd worked for the rest of his life—had decided to build himself this house, so he could come back to his hometown once and for all with his German wife. This German wife, whose name was Gudrun, was a widow with a twenty-year-old son called Ralf. Got that? Got it. Well, Angelo Speciale came down to Montereale in the company of his stepson Ralf and went around for a whole month looking for the right location. When he'd found it, and bought it, he went to see Michele Spitaleri, the developer, and had him draw up the plans. He waited over a year for the construction to be completed. Ralf stayed with him the whole time.

Then they went back to Germany to have all their furniture and other possessions shipped to Montereale. But a weird thing happened. Since this Angelo Speciale didn't like to fly, they went by train. When they got to Köln station, however, Signor Speciale couldn't find his stepson, who'd been traveling in the bunk over his. Ralf's suitcase was still in the compartment, but there was no trace of him. The night conductor said he hadn't seen anyone leave the train at any of the prior stops. In short, Ralf had disappeared.

"Did they ever find him?"

"Would you believe it, Inspector? They never did! From that moment on, nobody ever heard from the kid again!"

"And did Signor Speciale ever move into the house?"

"That's the best part! He never did! Poor Signor Speciale, he wasn't back in Cologne a month when he fell down the stairs, hit his head, and died!"

"What about the twice-widowed Signora Gudrun? Did she come down here to live?"

"What was she going to do here, poor thing, without her husband or son? She called us three years ago and told us to rent out the house. And since then we've been renting it, but only in the summer."

"Why not during the rest of the year?"

"It's too isolated, Inspector. You'll see for yourself."

It was indeed isolated. One got there by turning off the provincial road onto an uphill dirt road that had only a rustic little cottage, another slightly less rustic cottage, and, at the end, the house. There were hardly any trees or vegetation at all. The whole area was parched by the sun. But the moment one arrived at the house, which was at the top of a great big sort of hill, the view suddenly changed. It was breathtaking. Below, extending in both directions, was a beach of golden sand, dotted here and there by a few scattered umbrellas; and in front, a clear, open, welcoming sea. The house, which was all on one floor, had two bedrooms, a big one with a double bed and a smaller one with single bed, a spacious living room with rectangular windows looking onto nothing but sea and sky, not to mention a television. The kitchen was sizeable and equipped with an enormous refrigerator. There were even two bathrooms. And a terrace that was priceless, perfect for open-air dining in the evening.

"I like it," said the inspector. "How much is it?"

"Well, Inspector, normally we don't rent a house like this for only two weeks, but since it's for you . . ."

He spat out a figure that was like a billy-club to the head. But Montalbano didn't feel a thing. After all, Laura was plenty rich and could pay her part to alleviate the poverty of southern Italy.

"I like it," he repeated.

"Naturally, there will be some additional expenses—"

"Naturally, there *won't* be any additional expenses," said Montalbano, who didn't want to be taken for a fool.

"Okay, okay."

"How do you go down to the beach?"

"Well, you go through the little gate on the terrace, then walk about ten yards to a small stone staircase that leads down to the beach. There are fifty steps."

"Could you give me about half an hour?"

Callara looked befuddled.

"If you keep it to half an hour . . ." he said.

From the moment he'd seen it, Montalbano wanted to dive into that sea, which seemed to be beckoning him, and go for a long swim. He swam in his underpants.

When he returned, the sun had already dried him off during the time it took him to climb the fifty steps.

On the morning of the first of August, Montalbano went to Palermo's Punta Raisi airport to meet Livia, Laura, and her son, Bruno, a little boy of three. Guido, Laura's husband, would come later by train, bringing a car and their baggage across the Strait. Bruno was one of those little children incapable of sitting still for two consecutive minutes. Laura and Guido were a little concerned because the boy still didn't talk and communicated only by gestures. He didn't even like to draw or scribble, like other children his age; to make up for it, however, he was a master at busting the cojones of all creation.

They went to Marinella, where Adelina had prepared lunch for the whole gang. But Montalbano's housekeeper was already gone when they arrived, and Montalbano knew he wouldn't see her again for the remainder of Livia's fifteen days at Marinella. Adelina had a deep antipathy towards Livia, and the feeling was mutual.

Guido stumbled in around one o'clock. They ate, and immediately afterward, Montalbano got into his car with Livia to lead the way for Guido, in his car with his family. When Laura saw the house, she got so excited she hugged and kissed Montalbano. Bruno, too, gestured as if he wanted to be hugged by the inspector. But as soon as Montalbano raised him to his face, the boy spit the candy he was sucking into the inspector's eye.

They all agreed that the following morning, Livia would come to see Laura in Salvo's car, since he could get a ride to work in a squad car, and she would stay the whole day. That evening, when he got off work, Montalbano would have somebody drive him to Pizzo, and together they would decide where to go out to eat.

This seemed to the inspector an excellent solution, since it would allow him to feast on whatever he liked best at lunchtime, at Enzo's trattoria.

The troubles at the beachside house in Pizzo began on the morning of the third day. When she went to see her friend, Livia found the whole place turned upside down: clothes pulled out of the armoire and piled onto the chairs on the terrace, mattresses pushed up under the windows of the bedrooms, kitchen utensils strewn across the ground in the parking area in front of the entrance. Bruno, naked, with a garden hose in hand, was doing his best to soak all the clothes, mattresses, and sheets. He also tried to soak Livia the moment he saw her, but she, knowing him well, stepped out of the way. Laura was lying on a deck chair next to the low wall of the terrace, a wet rag over her forehead.

"What on earth is going on?"

"Have you been inside the house?"

"No."

"Look inside from the terrace, but be careful not to go in."

Livia went in through the little terrace gate, and looked into the living room.

The first thing she noticed was that the floor had turned almost black.

The second thing she noticed was that the floor was alive; that is, it was moving in all directions. After which she didn't notice anything else, having understood what it was she had seen. She only screamed and ran off the terrace.

"They're cockroaches! Thousands of them!"

"This morning, at the crack of dawn," Laura said with great effort, as if lacking even the breath to go on living, "I got up to get a drink of water, and I saw them. But there weren't so many of them yet . . . So I woke up Guido, and we tried to salvage whatever we could, but we quickly gave up. They kept coming up out of a crack in the living room floor . . ."

"And where's Guido now?"

"He went to Montereale. He called the mayor, who was very nice. He should be back at any moment."

"Why didn't he call Salvo?"

"He said he couldn't bring himself to call the police over an invasion of cockroaches."

Guido pulled up some fifteen minutes later, followed by a car from the mayor's office carrying four exterminators armed with poison canisters and brooms.

Livia took Laura and Bruno back to Marinella with her, while Guido stayed behind to coordinate the disinfestation and clean up the house. Around four o'clock in the afternoon, he too showed up at Marinella.

"They were coming straight up out of that crack in the floor. We sprayed two whole canisters down there, then cemented it up."

"There wouldn't happen to be any more of those cracks, would there?" Laura asked, seeming not very convinced.

"Don't worry, we looked everywhere very carefully," said Guido, settling the matter. "It won't happen again. We can go back home without fear."

"Who knows why they all came out like that . . ." Livia cut in.

"One of the exterminators explained that the house must have shifted imperceptibly during the night, causing the floor to crack. And the cockroaches, which were living underground, came up because they were attracted by the smell of food or by our presence. It's hard to say."

On the fifth day came the second invasion. Not of cockroaches, this time, but of little rodents. Laura, when she got up that morning, saw some fifteen of them, tiny little things, even sort of pretty. But they fled out the French doors to the terrace at high speed as soon as she moved. She found another two in the kitchen, munching away at some bread crumbs. Unlike most women, Laura was not deathly afraid of mice. Guido called the mayor again, drove into Montereale, and came back with two mousetraps, a quarter pound of sharp cheese, and a red cat, pleasant and patient—so patient,

11

in fact, that he didn't take offense when little Bruno immediately tried to gouge out one of his eyes.

"How can this be? First cockroaches climb up out of the floor, and now mice?" Livia asked Montalbano right after they got into bed.

With Livia lying naked next to him, Montalbano didn't feel like talking about rodents.

"Well, the house hadn't been lived in for a whole year . . ." was his vague reply.

"It probably should have been swept, scoured, and disinfected before Laura and her family moved in . . ." Livia concluded.

"I could use some of that myself," Montalbano cut in.

"Some of what?" asked Livia, confused.

"A good scouring."

And he kissed her.

On the eighth day came the third invasion. Again it was Laura, the first to get up, who noticed. She saw one out of the corner of her eye, jumped straight into the air, and, without knowing how, landed on top of the kitchen table, on her feet, eyes squeezed tightly shut. Then, when she felt it was safe enough, she slowly opened her eyes again, and, trembling and sweaty, looked down at the floor.

Where, in fact, some thirty spiders were blithely strolling along, as in a representative parade of the species: One was short and hairy, another had only a ball-like head on very long, wiry legs, a third was reddish and big as a crab, a fourth was the spitting image of the dreaded black widow ...

Laura, who was unfazed by cockroaches and unafraid of mice, did, on the other hand, fly into convulsions the moment she saw a spider. She suffered from what is called arachnophobia.

And so, with her hair standing straight on end, she let out an earsplitting scream and then fainted, plummeting from the table and onto the floor.

In her fall she hit her head, which began at once to bleed.

Woken up with a start, Guido bolted out of bed and rushed to his wife's rescue. But he didn't notice that Ruggero—that was the cat's name—was racing out of the kitchen, terrorized first by Laura's scream and then by the thud of her fall.

The upshot was that Guido suddenly found himself flying parallel to the ground until his head collided like a bumper with the refrigerator.

When Livia arrived at the usual hour to go for a swim with her friends, she walked into what looked like a field hospital.

Laura and Guido both had their heads wrapped in bandages, whereas Bruno's foot was all taped up, since, when he'd got out of bed he'd knocked a glass of water off the night table, shattering it to pieces, and then walked over the slivers of glass. Nonplussed, Livia noticed that even Ruggero the cat was limping slightly, as a result of his collision with Guido.

Lastly, the now familiar squad of exterminators arrived, sent by the mayor, who by this point had become a family friend. As Guido was overseeing operations, Laura, who still seemed upset, said to Livia under her breath:

"This house doesn't like us."

"Oh, come on. A house is a house. It doesn't have likes and dislikes."

"I'm telling you, this house doesn't like us."

"Oh, please."

"This house is cursed!" Laura insisted, her eyes sparkling as if she had a fever.

"Please, Laura, don't be silly. I realize your nerves are a little frayed, but—"

"You know, I'm beginning to reconsider all those films I've seen about haunted houses full of spirits that come up out of hell."

"But that's all make-believe!"

"I bet I'm right, just you wait and see."

On the morning of the ninth day, it started raining hard. Livia and Laura went to the Montelusa museum, and Guido was invited by the mayor to visit a salt mine and brought Bruno along with him. That night it rained even harder.

On the morning of the tenth day, it kept coming down in buckets. Laura phoned Livia to tell her she and Guido were taking Bruno to the hospital, because one of the cuts on his foot was beginning to ooze pus. Livia decided to take advantage of the circumstances to put Salvo's house in order. Late that evening the rain let up, and everyone was convinced that the following day would be clear and hot, a perfect day to spend on the beach.

2

Their prediction proved correct. The sea, no longer gray, had regained its usual color. The sand, being still wet, verged on light brown, but after two hours of sunlight it had turned back to gold. The water was perhaps a bit cool, but in that heat, which was already intense at seven in the morning, it would be warm as broth by midday. Which was the temperature Livia liked best. Whereas Montalbano couldn't stand it. It made him feel like he was swimming in a hot pool at a spa, and after he came out, he would feel sluggish and drained.

Arriving at Pizzo at nine-thirty, Livia was pleased to learn that it had been a normal morning so far, with no cockroaches, mice, or spiders, nor had there been any new arrivals of, say, scorpions or vipers. Laura, Guido, and Bruno were ready to go down to the beach.

As they were heading out through the little gate on the terrace, they heard the telephone ring inside the house. Guido, who was an engineer for a company specializing in bridge-building and had been receiving phone calls over the past two days concerning a problem he'd tried to explain to Montalbano with zero success, said:

"You all go on ahead. I'll join you in a minute."

And he went into the house to answer the phone.

"I need to pee," Laura said to Livia.

She went in, too. Livia followed behind. Because, for reasons unknown, the need to pee is contagious; all it takes is one person in a crowd needing to pee before everyone needs to. And so she went into the other bathroom.

When each had attended to his or her business, they met back up on the terrace. Guido locked the French doors as they filed out, closed the little gate behind them, grabbed the beach umbrella—which he, being the man, was obliged to carry—and they headed towards the little stone staircase that led down to the beach. Before they began their descent, however, Laura looked around and said:

"Where's Bruno?"

"Maybe he started going down by himself," said Livia.

"Oh my God, Bruno can't make it down by himself! I always have to hold his hand!" Laura said, looking a little worried.

They leaned out and looked down. From their vantage, they could see some twenty or so steps before the staircase turned. No sign of Bruno.

"He can't possibly have gone any farther down," said Guido.

"Go down and look, for heaven's sake! He may have fallen!" said Laura, who was beginning to get upset.

Guido rushed down the stairs with Laura's and Livia's eyes following him and disappeared around the turn. Not five minutes later, he reappeared round the curve.

"I went all the way down. He's not there. Go back and check the house. We may have locked him inside," he said in a high voice, panting hard.

"How will we do that?" said Laura. "You have the keys!"

Having hoped to spare himself the climb, Guido clambered up, cursing, opened the gate and then the French door. Then, all in chorus, they called:

"Bruno! Bruno!"

"That stupid kid is capable of lying hidden under a bed for a whole day just to spite us," said Guido, who was beginning to lose patience.

They searched for him all through the house, under the beds, inside the armoire, on top of the armoire, under the armoire, in the broom closet. Nothing doing. At a certain point, Livia said:

"But there's no sign of Ruggero, either . . ."

It was true. The cat, who was always getting tangled between one's feet—as Guido knew all too well—seemed to have disappeared, too.

"Usually he comes when we call him, or at least he meows. Let's try calling him," Guido suggested.

It was a logical idea. Since the kid couldn't talk, the only one who could respond in some way was the cat.

"Ruggero! Ruggero!"

No feline response.

"So Bruno must be outside," Laura surmised.

They all went out and searched around the house, even checking inside the two parked cars. Nothing.

"Bruno! Ruggero! Bruno! Ruggero!"

"Maybe he went walking down the little road that leads to the main one," Livia suggested.

Laura's reaction was immediate:

"But if he got that far . . . oh God, the traffic on that road is so awful!"

So Guido got into the car and drove very slowly down the dirt path leading to the main road, searching left and right. When he reached the end, he turned around and noticed that in front of the rustic cottage there now was a peasant of about fifty, poorly dressed, a dirty beret on his head, staring at the ground so intently that he seemed to be counting the ants.

Guido stopped and stuck his head out the window.

"Excuse me . . ."

"Eh?" said the man, raising his head and batting his eyelids like someone who had just woken up.

"Did you by any chance see a little boy pass this way?"

"Who?"

"A little three-year-old boy."

"Why?"

What kind of a question was that? wondered Guido, whose nerves by this point were on edge. But he answered:

"Because we can't find him."

"Ohh no!" said the fifty-year-old man, looking suddenly concerned and turning three-quarters away, towards his house.

Guido balked.

"What's that supposed to mean: 'Ohh no'?"

" 'Ohh no' means 'ohh no,' no? I never seen this little kid and anyhow I don't know nothing about 'im and I don't wanna know nothing 'bout none o' this business," he said firmly, then went into the house and closed the door behind him.

"Oh, no you don't! Hey, you!" said Guido, enraged. "That's no way to talk to people! Where are your manners?"

Spoiling for a fight and needing to let off some steam, he got out of the car, went and knocked on the door, even started kicking it. But it was hopeless. The door remained closed. Cursing to himself, he got back in the car, drove off, and passed by the other house, the one that looked a bit more decent. As it seemed empty, he continued back to their house.

"Nothing?"

"Nothing."

Laura threw herself into Livia's arms and started crying.

"See? Didn't I tell you this house was cursed?"

"Calm down, Laura, for heaven's sake!" her husband shouted.

The only result this obtained was to make Laura cry even harder.

"What can we do?" Livia asked.

Guido made up his mind.

"I'm going to call Emilio, the mayor."

"Why the mayor?"

"I'll have him send the usual squad. Or maybe some patrolmen. The more of us there are, the better. Don't you think?"

"Wait. Wouldn't it be better to call Salvo?"

"Maybe you're right."

Twenty minutes later, Salvo pulled up in a squad car driven by Gallo, who had raced there as if he was at Indianapolis.

Stepping out of the car, the inspector looked a bit haggard, pale, and aggrieved, but that was how he always looked after a ride with Gallo.

Livia, Guido, and Laura then proceeded to tell him what had happened, all at the same time, so that what little Montalbano was able to understand he grasped only by concentrating very hard. Then they stopped and waited for his answer—which was sure to be decisive—with the same expectation as pilgrims seeking grace from Our Lady of Lourdes.

"Could I have a glass of water?" was his anxiously awaited reply.

He needed to collect himself, either because of the tremendous heat or to recover from Gallo's prowess behind the wheel. While Guido went to get the water, the two women stared at him in disappointment.

"Where do you think he could be?" asked Livia.

"How should I know, Livia? I'm not a magician! Now we'll see what we can do. But stay calm, you two. All this agitation distracts me."

Guido handed him the water, and Montalbano drank it down.

"Could you please tell me what we're doing out here in

the sun?" he asked. "Getting sunstroke? Let's go inside. You come too, Gallo."

Gallo got out of the car and they all obediently followed the inspector.

But, for whatever reason, the minute they were in the living room, Laura's nerves gave out again. First she let out a shrill wail that sounded like a fire truck's siren, then started weeping uncontrollably. She'd had a sudden revelation.

"He's been kidnapped!"

"Try to be reasonable, Laura," said Guido, trying to call her back to her senses.

"But who would have kidnapped him?" Livia asked.

"How should I know? Gypsies! Albanians! Bedouins! I can feel that my poor little boy has been kidnapped!"

Montalbano had a wicked thought. If someone had in fact kidnapped a holy terror like Bruno, they would surely return him by the end of the day. Instead, he asked Laura:

"And why do you think they also kidnapped Ruggero?"

Gallo jumped out of his chair. He knew that one child had disappeared because the inspector had told him so; but after getting there he'd remained in the car and hadn't heard any of the things the others had told Montalbano. And now it came out that two were missing? He looked questioningly at his superior.

"Don't worry, he's a cat."

The idea of the cat had a miraculous effect. Laura seemed to calm down a little. Montalbano was opening his mouth to say what they needed to do when Livia tensed in her chair, goggled her eyes, and said in a flat voice:

"Oh my God, oh my God . . ."

They all looked at her, then turned their eyes in the direction she was looking.

In the living room doorway sat Ruggero the cat, calm and serene, licking his chops.

Laura let out another sirenlike wail and started screaming again.

"Can't you see that it's true? The cat is here and Bruno is not! He's been kidnapped! He's been kidnapped!"

Then she fainted.

Guido and Montalbano picked her up, carried her into the bedroom, and laid her down on the bed. Livia busied herself making cold compresses for Laura's forehead and put a bottle of vinegar under her nose. Nothing doing. Laura wouldn't open her eyes.

Her face was all gray, her jaw clenched, and she was drenched in a cold sweat.

"Take her into Montereale to see a doctor," Montalbano said to Guido. "You, Livia, go with them."

Having laid Laura down on the backseat of the car with her head on Livia's lap, Guido shot away at a speed that had even Gallo looking on in admiration. The inspector and Gallo then returned to the living room.

"Now that they're out of our hair," Montalbano said to him, "let's try to do something sensible. And the first sensible thing would be to put on our bathing suits. Otherwise, in this heat, we'll never manage to think clearly."

"I haven't got mine with me, Chief."

"Me neither. But Guido's got three or four."

23

They found them and put them on. Luckily they were elastic; otherwise the inspector would have needed suspenders and Gallo would have been charged with indecent exposure.

"Now, here's what we'll do. About ten yards past the little gate, there's a stone staircase that leads down to the beach. It's the only place, based on what I could gather from their confused story, where they didn't look closely, I think. I want you to go all the way down, but stop at every step. The kid may have fallen and rolled into some crevice in the rock."

"And what are you going to do, Chief?"

"I'm going to make friends with the cat."

Gallo looked at him dumbfounded, and went out.

"Ruggero!" the inspector called. "What a fine kitty you are! Ruggero!"

The cat rolled onto his back with his paws in the air. Montalbano tickled his belly.

"*Prrrrrr . . .*" said Ruggero.

"What do you say we go see what's in the fridge?" the inspector asked him, heading towards the kitchen.

Ruggero, who seemed not to object to the suggestion, followed him, and as Montalbano opened the refrigerator and pulled out two fresh anchovies, the cat rubbed against his legs, lightly butting his head.

The inspector took a paper plate, put the anchovies on it, set it down on the floor, waited for the cat to finish eating, then went outside onto the terrace. Ruggero, as he'd expected, came following after him. He headed towards the staircase, in time to see Gallo's head appear.

"Absolutely nothing, Chief. I could swear that the kid didn't go down these stairs."

"So, in your opinion, there's no way he could have gone down to the beach and into the water?"

"Chief, if I've understood correctly, the kid is three years old. He couldn't have done it even if he was running."

"So maybe we ought to do a better search of the surrounding area. There's no other explanation."

"Chief, what do you say we call the station and have a couple more men come for support?"

Gallo's sweat was dripping down to his feet.

"Let's wait just a little longer. Meanwhile, go cool yourself off. There's a hose in front of the house."

"But you yourself should put something on your head. Wait."

He went out on the terrace, where various beach accoutrements were scattered, and returned with Livia's hat, which was pink with a floral pattern.

"Here, put this on. What do you care? Nobody can see you here."

As Gallo went off, Montalbano noticed Ruggero was no longer with him. He went back into the house, to the kitchen, and called. No cat.

If he wasn't there licking the plate that had held the anchovies, then where could he have gone?

From what Laura and Guido had told him, he knew that the cat and the kid had become inseparable. Bruno, in fact, had made such a fuss, screaming and crying, that he'd succeeding in getting permission to have the cat sleep in his bed.

That was why Montalbano had made friends with Ruggero. He had a hunch that the cat knew exactly where the kid was.

And now, as he stood in the kitchen, it occurred to him that the cat had disappeared again because he'd gone back to see Bruno, to keep him company.

"Gallo!"

Gallo immediately appeared, getting water all over the floor.

"Your orders, Chief?"

"Listen, look in every room to see if the cat is in it. When you're sure he's not, close the window and door to that room, and do the same with the rest. We have to be sure the cat is nowhere in the house, and we have to prevent him from having any way to get back inside."

Gallo looked completely befuddled. Weren't they looking for a missing kid? Why had the inspector become so fixated on this cat?

"Excuse me, Chief, but what's the animal got to do with it?"

"Just do as I say. And leave only the front door open."

Gallo began his search, Montalbano went out through the little gate, walked to the edge of the cliff, which plunged straight down to the beach, then turned around to look at the house from that distance.

He studied it long and hard, until he became convinced that what he was seeing was not just an impression. Ever so imperceptibly, by only a few millimeters, the entire house listed to the left. It must certainly be the result of the ground's having shifted a few days earlier, causing the living room floor to crack and subsequently releasing the various invasions of cockroaches, mice, and spiders.

He went back to the terrace, grabbed a ball that Bruno had left on one of the deck chairs, and set it down on the ground. Slowly, the ball began to roll towards the little wall on the left.

It was the proof he was looking for. Which might explain everything or nothing at all.

Going back out through the little gate, he walked until he was far enough away to study the right side this time. All the windows on that wall were closed, which meant that Gallo had finished doing what he was supposed to do on that side. Montalbano saw nothing unusual.

Then he headed behind the house, where the entrance and the parking area were. The front door was open, as he'd told Gallo to leave it. Nothing out of the ordinary there.

He resumed walking until he could get a good look at the other side, the one where the house listed a little. The tilt was almost invisible. One of the two windows was closed, while the other was still open.

"Gallo!"

Gallo popped his head out.

"See anything?"

"This is the smaller bathroom. I'm done. The cat's not here. That leaves only the living room. Can I shut this window?"

As Gallo was closing the window, Montalbano noticed that the gutter above the window had broken, leaving a gap at least three fingers wide. It must have been an old problem that had never been fixed.

When it rained, all the rainwater poured out at that spot instead of going into the pipe that channeled it towards a well to one side of the terrace. To prevent a gigantic puddle from forming on the ground below and staining the wall of the house with humidity, somebody had put a big metal drum underneath it, one of those used for storing pitch.

Montalbano noticed, however, that the drum had been moved and was no longer perpendicular to the break in the gutter. It now stood at least three feet away from the wall.

If the water could no longer fall straight into the drum, Montalbano reasoned, then there should be a great big puddle here, a lake, since it had rained so hard over the last two days. Instead there was nothing. What was the explanation?

He felt a kind of electric shock, ever so slight, run down his spine. This usually happened to him when he was on the right track. He went up to the drum. There was, in fact, a bit of water in it, but not as much as there should have been, and it had certainly fallen there directly from the sky.

At that moment he noticed that the water pouring out of the gap in the gutter for two days and one night had carved out a veritable pit at the foot of the wall.

It was impossible at first to tell why the drum blocked it from view.

The pit had a circumference of about three feet. In all likelihood the surface of friable earth covering some sort of underground cavity had given way under the force of the water falling from above.

Montalbano removed Livia's hat, threw himself down flat on the ground, with his face practically inside the pit. Then he moved onto his side and stuck his arm into the opening, without, however, managing to touch the bottom. He realized that the pit did not descend vertically, but slantwise, along a sort of gentle incline.

He felt absolutely certain—and couldn't say why—that the kid had slipped into that pit and was no longer able to climb back out.

He stood up, ran wildly into the house, into the kitchen, opened the refrigerator, grabbed the platter full of anchovies, returned to the pit, knelt down, and began placing the anchovies one by one around the entrance.

At that moment Gallo arrived and saw the inspector—who, in the meantime, had put Livia's pink hat back on—sitting on the ground, his chest and arms soiled with dirt, staring intently at a hole in the ground ringed with anchovies.

He staggered, at a loss, stunned by the suspicion that his superior had gone out of his mind. What should he do? Humor him, the way one does with crazy people, to keep them calm?

"That's a really nice hole there, with all those anchovies around it," he said with an admiring smile, as if he were gazing at a work of modern art.

Montalbano gestured imperiously for him to shut up. Gallo fell silent, afraid the inspector, in his madness, might turn violent.

3

Five minutes later, they were both sitting there motionless. Gallo, too, had taken to staring, spellbound, at the anchovy-adorned pit, having caught the infectious intensity with which Montalbano kept his eye on it.

They looked as if sight was the only sense they had working, as if they'd turned all the other ones off and didn't hear the breath of the sea or smell the scent of a jasmine plant near the terrace.

Then, after what seemed to them like an eternity, out of the pit popped the head of Ruggero. He looked at Montalbano, uttered a *mrrrow* of thanks, and attacked the first anchovy.

"Holy shit!" exclaimed Gallo, having finally understood.

"I would bet my family jewels," said Montalbano, standing up, "that the kid is down there."

"Let's go find a shovel!" said Gallo.

"Don't be an idiot. The ground is so soft, it won't take but a minute to make it cave in."

"What'll we do?"

"You stay here and watch what the cat does. I'm gonna go call Fazio from the car."

"Fazio?"

"At your service, Chief."

"Listen, I'm with Gallo in the Pizzo district, at Montereale Marina."

"I know the place."

"There's a little kid, the son of some friends, who I think has fallen into a deep sort of pit in the ground and can't get out."

"I'll be right over."

"No. Call the fire chief of Montelusa. This is their sort of thing. Tell him the ground is very friable, and they should bring proper tools for digging and shoring up the walls. And, most importantly, no sirens, no noise at all. I don't want the media finding out. I don't want another Vermicino."

"Should I come, too?"

"No, there's no need."

He went into the house and called Livia's cell phone from the telephone in the living room.

"How's Laura doing?"

"She's asleep. They gave her a shot of tranquilizer. We were just getting into the car. What about Bruno?"

"I think I've located the spot where he is."

"Oh, God! What does that mean?"

"It means he fell into a pit where he can't get out."

"But . . . is he alive?"

"I don't know. I hope so. The firemen will be here soon. When the hospital discharges Laura, take her to our place in

Marinella. I don't want her here. Guido can come, if he wants."

"Keep me informed. I mean it."

He went back to Gallo, who hadn't moved.

"What did the cat do?"

"He ate all the anchovies and went into the house. Didn't you see him?"

"No. He must have gone into the kitchen to drink a little water."

Montalbano had noticed some time ago that he didn't hear as well as he used to. Nothing serious, but his hearing, like his vision, had dimmed. His ears used to be so keen he could hear the grass growing. Damned age!

"How's your hearing?" he asked Gallo.

"I got sharp ears, Chief."

"Try and see if you can hear anything."

Gallo lay flat on the ground, belly down, and stuck his head inside the pit.

"I think I heard something."

He covered his ears with his hands, took a deep breath, lowered his hands, then stuck his head into the pit again. Less than a minute later, he raised it and turned to look at Montalbano, a contented expression on his face.

"I heard him crying. I'm sure of it. He may've hurt himself when he fell. But it sounded really, really far away. How deep is this pit?"

"Well, injured or not, at least we know he's alive. And that's very good news."

At that moment Ruggero reappeared, said *mrrrow,* blithely hopped into the hole, and disappeared.

"He went to visit him," said the inspector.

Gallo made as if to get up, but Montalbano held him back.

"Wait a minute," he said. "Try and see if you can still hear the kid crying."

Gallo obeyed. He listened a long time, then said:

"No, I don't hear anything anymore."

"You see? Having Ruggero there comforts him."

"What do we do now?"

"Now I'm going into the kitchen to have myself a beer. You want one, too?"

"Nah, I think I'll have an orangeade. I saw some in the fridge."

They felt satisfied, even though they still had a long and difficult task ahead of them trying to pull the little boy out of the hole.

Montalbano drank his bottle of beer slowly, then called Livia.

"He's alive."

He told her the whole story. When he'd finished, Livia asked:

"Should I tell Laura?"

"Well, I don't think it's going to be so easy to pull him out, and the firemen aren't even here yet. You'd better not tell her anything yet. Is Guido still there with you?"

"No, he drove us to Marinella and now is on his way back to you."

One could immediately tell that the captain of the six-man squad of firemen was someone who knew how to do his job. Montalbano explained to him what he thought had happened, mentioned the shift in the ground that had occurred several days earlier, and told him of his impression that the house was listing slightly. The captain pulled out a spirit level and a plumb line and checked.

"You're right," he said. "It's listing."

Then he got down to work. First he tested the ground around the house with a sort of steel-tipped stick, then he looked around inside the house, stopping to examine the crack in the living room floor through which the cockroaches had entered, then he came back outside. He stuck a sort of flexible metal measuring tape into the pit, let it play out a long way, then rewound it, stuck it back in, then rewound it again. He was trying to find out how deep the pit might be.

"There's a sort of inclined plane in there," he said after doing some math, "which begins almost directly under the smaller bathroom window and ends under the window of the bedroom, about twenty feet down."

"You mean the depression runs the full length of this side of the house?" asked Guido.

"Exactly," said the fire chief. "Which is a very strange path for it to follow."

"Why?" asked Montalbano.

"Because if the depression was caused by rainwater, that means there is something underneath that diminished the water's force of penetration, preventing it from spreading entirely through the ground and being for the most part reabsorbed. The water came up against an obstacle, a kind of solid barrier, which forced it to follow an inclined plane."

"Can you handle it?"

"We need to proceed with extreme caution" was the fire chief's reply. "Because the soil surrounding the house is different from the rest; the slightest thing could make it give way."

"What do you mean, 'different from the rest'?" asked Montalbano.

"Follow me," the fire chief said.

He took some ten steps away from the house, with Montalbano and Guido following behind him.

"Look at the color of the soil here, then look how, ten yards up, near the house, it changes color. The soil we're standing on is natural to the place; that other soil, which is lighter and yellowish, is sandy. It was brought here deliberately."

"Why did they do that?"

"I have no idea," said the fire chief. "Maybe to make the house stand out, make it look more elegant. Ah, finally, here comes the mechanical shovel."

ANDREA CAMILLERI

Before putting the excavator to work, however, the fire chief wanted to lighten the weight of the sandy soil lying over the path of the depression. So, shovels in hand, three firemen started digging along the side of the house, dumping the dirt into three wheelbarrows, which their colleagues then emptied about ten yards away.

After they had removed about a foot of soil, they had a surprise. At the point where the house's foundations should have begun, there was a kind of second wall, perfectly plastered. To prevent the plaster from being damaged by humidity, sheets of plastic had been stuck to the wall to protect it.

In short, it was as if the house continued, all wrapped up, underground.

"All of you, dig down under the window of the smaller bathroom," the fire chief ordered.

And, little by little, the upper part of another window, perfectly aligned with the one above it, began to emerge. It had no casing in it, but was only a rectangular aperture with double sheets of plastic over it.

"There's another apartment down here!" said Guido in astonishment.

At this point, Montalbano suddenly understood everything.

"Stop digging!" he ordered.

Everyone stopped and looked at him questioningly.

"Has anyone got a flashlight?" he asked.

"I'll go get one!" said one of the firemen.

"Break the plastic over the window," the inspector further ordered.

Two jabs of the shovel sufficed. The firemen brought him the flashlight.

"You all wait here," Montalbano said, straddling the window.

He immediately no longer needed the flashlight, since the light coming in through the opening was more than enough.

He found himself inside a small bathroom, identical with the one on the floor above it. It was, moreover, a perfectly finished bathroom, with tiled floors and walls, a shower, sink, toilet, and bidet.

As he was looking around, wondering what this all could mean, something grazed against his leg, making him jump into the air from fright.

"Mrrrow," said Ruggero.

"Nice to see you again," said the inspector.

He turned on the flashlight and followed the animal into the room next door.

There, the weight of the water and soil had broken through the plastic over the window, turning the room into a bog.

And there was Bruno, standing in a corner, eyes shut tight. He had a cut on his forehead and was trembling all over as if he had malaria.

"Bruno, it's me, Salvo," the inspector said softly.

The little boy opened his eyes, recognized Montalbano, and ran to him, open-armed. The inspector embraced him, and Bruno started crying.

At that moment, Guido, who couldn't wait any longer, burst into the room.

███████

"Livia? Bruno's all right."

"Is he injured?"

"He has a cut on his forehead, but I don't think it's serious. In any case, Guido is taking him to the emergency room in Montereale. Tell Laura and, if it's all right with her, you should accompany her there. I'll wait for you all here."

███████

Straddling the window through which Montalbano had entered, the fire chief came out. He looked bewildered.

"There's a whole apartment down here, exactly like the one upstairs. There's even a terrace with a railing around it! All you'd have to do is install the internal and external casings, which are stacked in the living room, and you could move right in! There's even running water! And the electrical system is all ready to be hooked up! What I don't understand is why they buried everything underground."

Montalbano, for his part, had a very precise idea of why they'd done it.

"I think I know why. I'm sure they were originally granted a permit for a house without an upstairs. But the owner, in league with the builder and the work foreman, had the house built exactly the way we see it now. Then he had the ground floor completely covered with sandy soil, so that only the upstairs remained visible, turning it into the ground floor."

"Yes, but why did he do it?"

"He was waiting for amnesty on code violations. The moment the government approved it, he would remove all the dirt covering the other apartment overnight, then put in his request for amnesty. Otherwise he risked having the whole thing demolished, even though that's very unlikely around here."

The fire chief started laughing.

"Demolished? Around here there are entire towns built illegally!"

"Yes, but I found out that the owner lived in Germany. It's possible he forgot about our wonderful ancient customs and thought that people respected the law here the way they do in Cologne."

The fire chief looked unconvinced.

"Okay, but this government has granted one amnesty after another! Why, then—"

"I found out he died a few years ago."

"What should we do? Put everything back the way it was?"

"No, leave everything just the way it is now. Could that create any problems?"

"For the upstairs, you mean? No, none whatsoever."

"I want to show this fine handiwork to the owner of the agency that rented out the house."

Left alone, the inspector took a shower, dried himself off in the sun, then got dressed. He grabbed another bottle of beer. He had worked up a serious appetite. What was taking the gang so long?

"Hello, Livia? Are you still in the emergency room?"

"No, we're on our way. Bruno's fine, there's nothing wrong with him."

He hung up and dialed the number of Enzo's trattoria.

"Montalbano here. I know it's late and you're about to close, but if I came with a party of four plus a little kid, think we could still get something to eat?"

"For you, Inspector, we're always open."

As always happens, the narrow escape made everyone so giddy and ravenous that Enzo, hearing them laughing and eating nonstop as if they'd just broken a weeklong fast, asked what they were celebrating. Bruno acted as if he'd been bitten by a tarantula, continually jumping about, knocking first the cutlery off the table, then a glass that luckily didn't break, and, last, spilling a bottle of olive oil all over Montalbano's pants. For a brief moment the inspector regretted having been so quick to pull him out of that hole in the ground. But he immediately felt guilty for having the thought. When everyone had finished eating, Livia and her friends drove back to Pizzo. Montalbano, on the other hand, raced home to change his pants, then went to the office to work.

That evening, he asked Fazio if there was a squad car available to take him home.

"There's Gallo, Chief."

"Nobody else?"

He wanted to avoid another Indianapolis-style dash like the one he'd endured in the morning.

"No, sir."

Once in the car, he admonished Gallo.

"Listen, Gallo. We're in no hurry this time. Drive slowly."

"Tell me how fast you want me to go, Chief."

"Twenty miles per hour, max."

"Twenty?! Chief, I don't even *know* how to drive twenty miles an hour. I'm liable to crash into something. What do you say we go thirty-five, forty?"

"Okay."

Everything went smoothly until they turned off the main road and onto the unpaved one leading to the house. Right in front of the rustic cottage, a dog dashed in front of them. To avoid him, Gallo swerved and nearly crashed into the cottage's front door, shattering an earthenware jug that was beside it.

"You broke something," said Montalbano.

As they were getting out of the car, the door to the cottage opened and the peasant of about fifty appeared, still wearing shabby clothes and a dirty beret on his head.

"What happened?" asked the man, turning on a small light over the door.

"We broke your jug and wanted to compensate you for the damage," Gallo said politely.

Then something strange happened. The man looked at the squad car, turned around, extinguished the light, went back in the house and locked the door. Gallo looked puzzled.

"He saw the police car," said Montalbano. "Apparently he doesn't like us. Try knocking."

Gallo knocked. Nobody came to the door.

"Hey! Anybody home?"

Nobody answered.

"Let's get out of here," said the inspector.

Laura and Livia had set the table on the terrace. The evening was so beautiful it was heartbreaking. The heat of the day had mysteriously given way to a restorative cool, and the moon floating over the sea was so bright that they could have eaten by its light alone.

The two women had prepared light fare, since they'd gone late to Enzo's and had stuffed themselves into the bargain.

As they were sitting around the table, Guido told the others what had transpired that morning between him and the peasant from the rustic cottage.

"As soon as I said a little boy had disappeared, he said 'Ohh no' and ran and shut himself up in the house. I knocked and knocked, but he wouldn't open."

So it's not just the police he has problems with, thought the inspector. But he didn't say anything about the nearly identical treatment he himself had received.

After they'd eaten, Guido and Laura suggested they all go for a walk on the beach in the moonlight. Livia declined, and so did Montalbano. Luckily Bruno chose to go with his parents.

After they'd been sitting for a while in the deck chairs, enjoying a silence broken only by the purring of Ruggero, who was luxuriating in the inspector's lap, Livia said:

"Would you show me the place where you found Bruno? You know, ever since we've been back, Laura has forbidden me to go see where he fell."

"All right. Let me get a flashlight. There's one in the car."

"Guido must also have one somewhere. I'll see if I can find it."

They met back up in front of the excavated window, each with a flashlight in hand. Montalbano climbed through the opening first, checked to make sure there weren't any rats, then helped Livia inside. Naturally, Ruggero hopped in after them.

"Unbelievable!" said Livia, looking at the bathroom.

The air was damp and heavy. The only window through which any fresh air could enter was not enough to ventilate the space. They went into the room where the inspector had found Bruno.

"You'd better not go any further, Livia. It's a swamp."

"The poor boy! He must have been so scared!" said Livia, heading towards the living room.

In the beam of the flashlights they saw the window frames, all wrapped up in plastic. Montalbano noticed a rather large trunk pushed up against a wall. Overcome by curiosity, he opened it, since it wasn't locked.

At that moment he looked exactly like Cary Grant in *Arsenic and Old Lace*. He quickly slammed the trunk shut and sat down on top of it. When the beam from Livia's flashlight shone on his face, he automatically smiled.

"What are you smiling about?"

"Me? I'm not smiling."

"So why are you making that face?"

"What face?"

"What's in the trunk?" Livia asked.

"Nothing. It's empty."

How could he possibly have told her there was a corpse inside?

4

When Guido and Laura returned from their romantic stroll along the moonlit beach, it was past eleven.

"That was amazing!" Laura exclaimed enthusiastically. "I really needed that, after a day like today."

Guido was a little less enthusiastic, given that halfway through their walk, Bruno had suddenly become very sleepy, and he'd had to carry him in his arms the rest of the way.

Ever since he'd sat back down in the deck chair after visiting the phantom apartment with Livia, Montalbano had been beset with a dilemma worse than Hamlet's: to tell or not to tell?

If he did tell them there was a corpse downstairs, indescribable chaos would break out and the rest of the night would be hell, or almost. It was more than certain, in fact, that Laura would adamantly refuse to spend one minute more under the same roof as an unknown corpse and demand to sleep somewhere else.

But where? At Marinella there wasn't even a guest room. They would have to camp out. And how would they do that? He imagined how they would work things out, with Laura,

Livia, and Bruno in the double bed, Guido on the sofa, and himself in the armchair. He shuddered.

No, that was no solution. Better a hotel. But where, at midnight, in Vigàta, were they going to find a hotel still open? Maybe Montelusa was a better bet. Which would mean phone call after phone call, back and forth in the car, to and from Montelusa, to keep their friends company, and, as icing on the cake, the inevitable all-night argument with Livia.

"But why did you have to choose *that* house?"

"Livia, darling, how was I to know there was a dead body in it?"

"How were you to know? What kind of policeman are you anyway?"

No, he decided, it was better, for now, to say nothing to anyone.

After all, God only knew how long the corpse had been in that trunk. One day more or one day less wasn't going to make any difference. Nor would it affect the investigation in any way.

Having said good-bye to their friends, then, Livia and the inspector headed back to Marinella.

The moment Livia went to take a shower, Montalbano, from the terrace, called Fazio on the cell phone, keeping his voice down.

"Fazio? Montalbano here."

"What's wrong, Chief?"

"I haven't got time to explain. In ten minutes, I want you to call me back at home and say you urgently need me to come in to the station."

"Why, what's happened?"

"Don't ask questions. Just do as I say."

"Then what do I do afterward?"

"You hang up and go back to sleep."

Five minutes later Livia emerged from the bathroom and Montalbano went in. As he was brushing his teeth, he heard the telephone ring. As expected, Livia went to pick up. This would make the whole scene he had staged more credible.

"Salvo, it's Fazio on the phone!"

He went into the dining room with his toothbrush still in his mouth, lips frothing with toothpaste, muttering to himself for Livia's benefit, as she glared at him:

"Can't anyone get a little peace and quiet around here, even at this hour?"

He grabbed the phone gruffly:

"What is it?"

"You're needed down at the station at once."

"Can't you guys handle it yourselves? No? Okay, okay, I'll be right there."

He slammed the receiver down hard, feigning anger:

"Won't those guys ever grow up? Do they always need Daddy's help? I'm sorry, Livia, but, unfortunately I—"

"I understand," said Livia in a tone straight from the polar ice caps. "I'm going to bed."

"Will you wait up for me?"

"No."

He got dressed, went out, got in the car, and headed to Marina di Montereale.

He drove extremely slowly, because he wanted to waste as much time as possible, to be more or less certain that Laura and Guido had gone to bed.

When he got to Pizzo, he went as far as the second house—the uninhabited but well-maintained one—stopped, and got out, bringing the flashlight with him. He traveled the remaining stretch of the dirt road on foot, afraid that if he came any closer with the car, the sound, in the stillness of the night, might wake up his friends.

No light shone in any of the windows, a good sign that Laura and Guido were well on their way to dreamland.

With a light step he sidled up to the window that served as a door, climbed through, and went in. When he was inside, he turned on the flashlight and headed towards the living room.

He lifted the trunk's lid. The corpse was barely visible, having been wrapped several times over in the same kind of plastic sheets that had been used to seal off the secret apartment, and then bound in brown packing tape wound many times around the bundle. The corpse looked like a cross between a mummy and a giant parcel ready for shipping.

He shone the flashlight closer and realized, at least from what he was able to see, that the body was fairly well preserved. Apparently all that plastic had created a sort of hard vacuum, not allowing even a trace of the terrible stench of death to leak out.

Forcing himself to look harder, he noticed a great mass of long blond hair on and around the head. The face, on the other hand, he couldn't make out, because it had been wrapped twice around with the brown adhesive tape.

It was a woman, that much was clear.

There was nothing more to see or do. He closed the trunk, exited the apartment, got back in his car, and drove home.

He found Livia in bed but still awake. She was reading a book.

"Darling, I got back as quickly as I could. I'll just take the shower I wasn't able to—"

"Go on, hurry. Don't waste any more time."

When Livia came out of the bathroom at nine o'clock the following morning, she found Montalbano sitting on the veranda.

"What, are you still here? You told me you had to go to the station to deal with that business of last night."

"I've changed my mind. I'm going to take a half day's vacation. I'm coming with you to Pizzo to spend the morning with you and your friends."

"Oh, goody!"

By the time they got there Laura, Guido, and Bruno were ready to go down to the beach. Since they had decided they would spend the whole day outside, Laura had filled some baskets with food.

But how and when—the inspector anxiously wondered in the meantime—was he going to break the good news to them?

As luck would have it Guido helped him out.

"Did you call the people at the agency to tell them about the illegal apartment?"

"No, not yet."

"Why not?"

"Because I'm afraid they might raise your rent, since you now have another apartment at your disposal."

He was trying to make a joke of it, but Livia intervened.

"Come on, what are you waiting for? I want to see the look on the face of the guy that rented it to you."

And I can't wait to see yours, in a few minutes! thought Montalbano.

But he said instead:

"Well, there's a major complication."

"What?"

"Could you send Bruno away for a minute?" Montalbano asked Laura under his breath.

She gave him a puzzled look, but did as he said.

"Bruno, do Mommy a little favor. Go in the kitchen and get another bottle of mineral water from the refrigerator."

The others stared at him, their curiosity aroused by his question.

"So?"

"The fact is, I found a dead body. A woman."

"Where?" Guido asked.

"In the apartment downstairs. In the living room. Inside a trunk."

"Are you joking?" asked Laura.

"No, he's not joking," said Livia. "I know him well. Did you discover it last night, when we went down there?"

Bruno returned carrying a bottle.

"Go get another!" they all said in unison.

The child set the bottle down on the floor and ran out.

"And you," said Livia, who was beginning to understand what was happening, "you let my friends spend the night here with a dead body in the house?"

"Come on, Livia! It's downstairs! It's not contagious!"

All of a sudden, Laura let out her siren wail, which had become her specialty.

Ruggero, who had been sunning himself on the little wall, hightailed it away. Bruno returned, set the second bottle on the floor, and ran to get another without anyone's having asked him.

"You're such a jerk!" Guido said angrily, following after his wife, who had run weeping into the bedroom.

"But I did what I thought was best!" said Montalbano, trying to justify himself in Livia's eyes.

She only looked at him in disdain.

"When Fazio phoned you last night, you had already arranged with him to provide you with an excuse to go out, hadn't you?"

"Yes."

"And did you come back here to have a better look at the corpse?"

"Yes."

"And afterwards you made love to me! You are an animal! A brute!"

51

ANDREA CAMILLERI

"But I took a shower so that—"

"You're a repulsive creature!"

She got up, leaving him standing there, and went into her friends' bedroom. She returned about five minutes later, cold as ice.

"They're packing their bags."

"They're leaving? What about the plane tickets?"

"Guido decided not to wait any longer. They're going to go by car. Take me back to Marinella. I need to pack, too, because I'm going with them."

"Oh, Livia, try to be reasonable!"

"I don't want to hear another word!"

It was hopeless. On the drive back to Marinella, she didn't open her mouth and Montalbano didn't dare. As soon as they got there, Livia threw her things helter-skelter into her suitcase, then went out and sat on the veranda with a long face.

"You want me to fix you something to eat?"

"You only think of two things."

She didn't say what those two things were, but Montalbano understood anyway.

Around one o'clock, Guido arrived to pick up Livia. Also in the car was Ruggero, with whom Bruno had apparently refused to part. Guido handed the house keys over to Montalbano, but did not shake his hand. Laura kept her head turned away, Bruno gave him a Bronx cheer, and Livia wouldn't even kiss him good-bye.

Rejected and abandoned, Montalbano watched them

leave with a heavy heart. But also, deep down, with a sense of relief.

The first thing he did was phone Adelina.

"Adelì, Livia had to go back to Genoa. Could you come tomorrow morning?"

"Yes, signore. I can even come in a couple a hours."

"That's all right, there's no need."

"No, signore, Ima gonna come anyways. I can just imagina mess Miss Livia lefta house in!"

There was a little bit of hard bread left in the kitchen. Montalbano ate it with a slice of tumazzo cheese that was in the fridge. Then he lay down in bed and fell asleep.

When he woke up it was four o'clock. He could hear from the tinkle of plates and glasses in the kitchen that Adelina had already arrived.

"Could you bring me a cup of coffee, Adelì?"

"Right away, signore."

She brought the coffee with a scowl on her face.

"*Madonna mia!* The plates was all covered with grease an' I even foun' a pair a dirty unnerpants in the batroom!"

Now, in reality, if there was a fanatically neat woman in the world, it was Livia. But in Adelina's eyes, she had always seemed like someone whose ideal was to live in a pigsty.

"But I told you, she had to leave in a hurry."

"You have a fight? You break up?"

"No, we didn't break up."

Adelina seemed disappointed and went back in the kitchen.

Montalbano got up to make a phone call.

"Aurora Agency? Inspector Montalbano here. I'd like to speak with Signor Callara."

"I'll put him on right away," replied a woman's voice.

"Inspector? Good afternoon, what can I do for you?"

"Are you in the office for the day?"

"Yes, I'll be here till we close. Why?"

"I'll be by in half an hour to return the keys to the beach house."

"What? Weren't they supposed to stay until—"

"Yes, but my friends were forced to leave this morning. A sudden death. Unfortunately they couldn't stay the whole time."

"Listen, Inspector, I don't know if you read the contract."

"I glanced at it. Why?"

"Because it states clearly that the client gets nothing back in the event of an early departure."

"Who asked for anything back, Signor Callara?"

"Ah, okay. Well, then don't bother coming here yourself. I'll send someone down to the station to pick up the keys."

"I need to talk to you and then show you something."

"Come by whenever you like."

———

"Catarella? Montalbano here."

"I already rec'nize ya inasmuch as yer voice is all yours, Chief."

"Any news?"

"No sir, Chief, nuttin. 'Xcept fer Filippo Ragusano, you know him, Chief, he's a one wherats got a shoe store by the church, and 'e shot 'is brother-n-law Gasparino Manzella."

"Did he kill him?"

"Nossir, Chief, jess grazed 'im."

"Why'd he shoot him?"

"Says Gasparino Manzella was gettin on 'is noives since it was rilly hot 'n all an' a fly was walkin on 'is head which rilly bugged 'im an' so he shot 'im."

"Fazio there?"

"Nossir, Chief. 'E went out by the iron bridge 'cuz some guy busted 'is wife's head out that way."

"Okay. I wanted to tell you—"

"But there's somethin else happened."

"Oh, yeah? I was somehow under the impression that nothing had happened. What happened?"

"What happened izzat Corporeal 'Tective Alberto Virduzzo went into a muddy locality and slipped wit' both 'is legs in the mud that was there, breaking one o' the legs aforesaid. Gallo took 'im to the hospitable."

"Listen, I wanted to tell you that I'll be late coming in."

"You're the boss, Chief."

Signor Callara was busy with a client. Montalbano stepped outside to smoke a cigarette in the open air. It was so hot that the asphalt was starting to melt, making one's shoes stick slightly to it. Once Callara was free, he came out in person to meet Montalbano.

"Please come into my office, Inspector. I've got air-conditioning."

Which Montalbano hated. Never mind.

"Before I take you to see something—"

"Where do you want to take me?"

"To the house you rented to my friends."

"Why? Is there anything wrong? Anything broken?"

"No, everything's fine. But I think you should come."

"As you wish."

"I believe I remember you saying, when you took me to see the house, that it was a man who had emigrated to Germany that had the house built. A certain Angelo Speciale, who had married a German widow, whose son, Ralf, I think you said, had come here with his father-in-law and then mysteriously disappeared on their way back to Germany. Is that correct?"

Callara looked at him in admiration.

"Absolutely. What a memory you've got!"

"You, naturally, have the name, address, and telephone number of Signora Speciale?"

"Of course. Wait just one minute while I look for the information on Signora Gudrun."

Montalbano wrote it all down on a scrap of paper. Callara became curious.

"For what purpose—"

"You'll understand later. I seem also to remember that

you gave me the name of the developer who designed the house and oversaw the construction."

"Yes. His name is Michele Spitaleri. Would you like his phone number?"

"Yes."

Montalbano jotted that down, too.

"Listen, Inspector. Can't you tell me why—"

"I'll tell you on the way there. Here's the key. Keep it with you."

"Will this take long?"

"I couldn't say."

Callara gave him an inquisitive look. Montalbano donned an expressionless mask.

"Maybe I'd better tell the secretary," said Callara.

They headed off in Montalbano's car. On the way, the inspector told Callara how little Bruno had disappeared, how hard it had been to find him, and finally how they'd pulled him out with the help of the firemen.

Callara was worried about one thing only.

"Did they do any damage?"

"Who?"

"The firemen. Did they damage the house in any way?"

"No, not inside."

"That's a relief. 'Cause one time when a fire broke out in the kitchen of a house I'd rented, they did more damage than the fire."

Not a word about the illegal apartment.

"Do you intend to inform Signora Gudrun?"

"Of course, of course. But she certainly doesn't know anything about this. It must have been an idea of Angelo Speciale's. I'll have to take care of everything myself."

"Are you going to apply for amnesty?"

"Well, I don't know if—"

"Look, Signor Callara, don't forget I'm a public official. I can't just look the other way."

"What if—just supposing, mind you—what if I inform Spitaleri and have everything put back the way it was—"

"Then I will charge you, Signora Gudrun, and Spitaleri with illegal construction."

"Well, if that's the way it is . . ."

▬▬

"Look at that! Look at that!" was Signor Callara's exclamation of wonderment as he entered through the bathroom window and saw everything ready for use.

With flashlight in hand, Montalbano led him into the other rooms.

"Look at that! Look at that!"

They arrived in the living room.

"Look at that! Look at that!"

"See?" said Montalbano. "Even the casings are ready for installation."

"Look at that! Look at that!"

As if by chance, the inspector let the beam of the flashlight fall upon the trunk.

"And what's that?" asked Callara.

"Looks like a trunk to me."

"What's inside? Have you opened it?"

"Me? No. Why would I have done that?"

"Would you lend me the flashlight a minute?"

"Here."

Everything was going as planned.

Callara opened the trunk, and when he aimed the beam inside, he did not say "Look at that," but took a great leap backwards.

"Ohmygod! Ohmygod!"

The beam of the flashlight trembled in his hand.

"What is it?"

"But . . . but . . . there's a . . . there's a . . . dead person!"

"Really?"

5

Thus, with the dead body's deadness now official, the inspector could look into doing something about it.

First, however, he had to do something about Signor Callara, who, having dashed outside through the window, was now vomiting up what he had eaten the week before.

Montalbano opened the real apartment upstairs, made Signor Callara, who was feeling very dizzy, lie down on the sofa in the living room, and went to get him a glass of water.

"Can I go home?"

"Are you kidding? I can't drive you home."

"I'll call my son and have him come get me."

"Not on your life! You have to wait for the public prosecutor! It was you who discovered the body, no? Would you like a little more water?"

"No, I feel cold."

Cold? In this heat?

"I've got a blanket in the car. I'll go get it."

His role as Good Samaritan over, he called the station.

"Catarella? Is Fazio there?"

"He'll be comin soon."

"What does that mean?"

"He phoned just now sayin zackly: I'll be there in five minutes. What I mean is, *he* will be here in five minutes, not me, since I'm already here."

"Listen, a dead body's been found, and I want him to call me at this number."

He gave him the telephone number of the house.

"Hee, hee!" said Catarella.

"Are you laughing or crying?"

"Laughin, Chief."

"Why's that?"

" 'Cause normalwise iss always me tellin you when summon finds a dead body, an' now iss you tellin me!"

Five minutes later, the telephone rang.

"What is it, Chief? You find a dead body?"

"The head of the agency that rented the apartment to my friends found it. Luckily they'd already left before this wonderful discovery was made."

"Is it fresh?"

"I don't think so. In fact, I would rule that out. But I didn't get a good look at it, 'cause I had to give a hand to Signor Callara, poor guy."

"So, it's the same house where I sent the firemen?"

"Exactly. Marina di Montereale, Pizzo district, the house at the end of the dirt road. Bring some support. And inform the prosecutor, Forensics, and Dr. Pasquano. I don't feel like doing it myself."

"I'll be right over, Chief."

As he was putting on his gloves, Fazio, who'd come with Galluzzo, asked Montalbano:

"Can I go down and have a look?"

The inspector was reclining in a deck chair on the terrace, enjoying the sunset.

"Sure. Be careful not to leave any fingerprints."

"You're not coming?"

"What for?"

Half an hour later, the usual pandemonium broke out.

First the Forensics team arrived, but since they couldn't see a goddamn thing in the underground living room, they lost another half hour setting up a temporary electrical connection.

Then Pasquano arrived with the ambulance and his team of undertakers. Realizing immediately that he would have to wait his turn, the doctor pulled up another deck chair, sat down beside the inspector, and dozed off.

An hour or so later, by which time the sun had almost entirely set, someone from Forensics came and woke him up.

"Doctor," he said, "the body's all wrapped up. What should we do?"

"Unwrap it" was the laconic reply.

"Yes, but who should do the unwrapping, us or you?"

"I guess I'd better unwrap it myself," said Pasquano with a sigh.

"Fazio!" Montalbano called out.

"Reporting, Chief."

"Has Prosecutor Tommaseo arrived yet?"

"No, Chief, he called to say it would take him at least an hour to get here."

"You know what I say?"

"No, sir."

"I say I'm gonna go eat and come back. Looks to me like things are gonna take a long time."

Passing through the living room, he noticed that Callara hadn't moved from the sofa. He took pity on him.

"Come with me, I'll give you a lift to Vigàta. I'll tell the prosecutor how things went."

"Oh, thank you, thank you," said Callara, handing him the blanket.

He dropped Callara off in front of his agency, which was now closed.

"Don't forget: Not a word to anyone about the corpse you found."

"My dear Inspector, I think I'm running a fever of a hundred and two. I don't even feel like breathing, let alone talking!"

Since going to Enzo's would surely take too long, he headed back to Marinella instead.

In the fridge he found a rather sizeable platter of caponata and a big piece of Ragusan caciocavallo cheese. Adelina had even bought him some fresh bread. He was so hungry, his eyes were burning.

It took him a good hour to polish it all off, to the accompaniment of half a liter of wine. Then he washed his face, got in his car, and drove back to Pizzo.

The moment the inspector arrived, Tommaseo, the public prosecutor, who'd been standing in the parking area in front of the house getting a breath of air, came running up to him.

"It looks like a sex-related crime!"

His eyes were sparkling, his tone almost festive. That's how Prosecutor Tommaseo was: Any crime of passion, any killing related to infidelity or sex, was pure bliss for him. Montalbano was convinced he was a genuine maniac, but only in his mind.

Tommaseo would drool like a snail after every woman he interrogated, and yet nobody knew of any female friends or lovers in his life.

"Is Dr. Pasquano still inside?" asked Montalbano.

"Yes."

It was stifling in the illegal apartment. Too many people going in and out, too much heat given off by the two floodlights the Forensics team had turned on. The already close atmosphere of before was a lot closer, with the difference that now it stank of men's sweat, and now, indeed, one also smelled the stench of death.

The corpse had, in fact, been taken out of the trunk, unwrapped as best as was possible, considering that one could see pieces of the plastic still sticking to the skin, having perhaps fused with it over time. The men had placed the body, naked as they'd found it, on a stretcher, and Dr. Pasquano, cursing under his breath, was finishing his examination. Montalbano realized that it wasn't a good time to ask him anything.

"Get me the prosecutor!" the doctor suddenly ordered.

Tommaseo came in.

"Listen, Judge, I can't go on working in here. It's too hot, the thing's liquefying before my eyes. Can I take it away?"

Tommaseo looked inquiringly at the head of Forensics, Vanni Arquà.

"If you ask me, yes," said Arquà.

Arquà and Montalbano got on each other's nerves. They didn't say hello when they met, and they spoke to one another only in cases of pure necessity.

"Okay, take the body out of here and put seals over the window," Tommaseo ordered.

Pasquano looked at Montalbano. Without saying anything to anyone, the inspector went back upstairs, took a bottle of beer from the fridge—Guido had restocked—and returned to the terrace, settling into the same deck chair. He heard the noise of cars leaving.

A few minutes later Dr. Pasquano appeared, and sat down as before.

"I see you know the house well. Could I have a beer, too?"

As the inspector was headed towards the kitchen, Fazio and Galluzzo came in.

"Chief, can we go now?"

"Sure. Here, take this piece of paper. It's the phone number of a developer named Michele Spitaleri. I want you to track him down, right now; you absolutely have to find him and tell him that I'll be waiting for him at the station tomorrow morning at nine o'clock sharp. Good night."

He brought the cold beer out to Pasquano and told him how and why he knew the house so well. Then he said:

"Doctor, it's too beautiful an evening to get you pissed off. You tell me if you want to answer a few of my questions or not."

"No more than four or five."

"Did you manage to determine her age?"

"Yes. She was probably fifteen or sixteen years old. That's one."

"Tommaseo told me it was a sex-related crime."

"Tommaseo is a perverted asshole. That's two."

"What do you mean, two? You can't count that as a question! Don't cheat! We're still on the first one!"

"Oh, all right."

"Second question: Was she raped?"

"I'm not in a position to say. Maybe not even after the autopsy. Although I would assume she was."

"Third: How was she killed?"

"They cut her throat."

"Four: How long ago?"

"Five or six years. She was well preserved because they wrapped her up well."

"Five: In your opinion, was she killed down there or somewhere else?"

"You should ask Forensics. Whatever the case, Arquà found plenty of traces of blood on the floor."

"Six—"

"No, no, no! Time's up and beer's finished. Good night."

He got up and left. Montalbano also stood up, but only to get himself another beer in the kitchen.

He didn't have the heart to leave the terrace on a night like this. All of a sudden, he missed Livia. Just the previous evening, they'd been sitting in this exact same place, in harmony and in love.

Suddenly the night felt cold to him.

Fazio was already at the station by eight o'clock the next morning. Montalbano arrived half an hour later.

"Chief, you gotta forgive me, but I just don't believe it."

"You just don't believe what?"

"The story of how the body was discovered."

"How else was it supposed to have been discovered, Fazio? Callara happened to see the trunk, he lifted the lid, and—"

"Chief, if you ask me, you arranged things so that Callara would be the one to open it."

"Why would I do that?"

"Because you'd already found the body the day before, when you went to get the kid. You've got a nose like a hunting dog, Chief! Like you're not going to open that trunk! And you didn't say anything right away so your friends could leave in peace."

He had understood everything. That wasn't exactly the way things had gone, but by and large Fazio was right on the mark.

"Listen, you can believe whatever you like. Did you find Spitaleri?"

"I tried him at home and his wife gave me his cell phone number. At first there was no answer because it was turned off, but then, an hour later, he picked up. He'll be here at nine o'clock sharp."

"Find out anything?"

"Of course, Chief."

He pulled a little piece of paper out of his pocket and started reading.

"Michele Spitaleri, son of Bartolomeo Spitaleri and Maria Finocchiaro, born in Vigàta on November 6, 1960, and currently residing in said city, on via Lincoln 44, married to—"

"That's enough," said Montalbano. "I let you get it out of your system for a second, because I felt like being nice today, but now that's enough."

"Thanks for being nice," said Fazio.

"Tell me who this Spitaleri is."

"Well, seeing as how his sister married Pasquale Alessandro, and seeing as how Alessandro has been mayor of Vigàta for the last eight years, this Spitaleri happens to be the mayor's brother-in-law."

"Elementary, my dear Watson."

"Owning, in that capacity, three construction companies and being a surveyor by trade, he gets ninety percent of the municipality's contracts."

"And they let him do that?"

"Yes they do, because he pays his dues in equal part to both the Cuffaros and the Sinagras. And naturally, he kicks back a cut to his brother-in-law."

And therefore, since the Cuffaros and the Sinagras were the two dominant Mafia families in the area, the developer could consider himself safe.

"So the final cost of every contract ends up being double the figure established at the outset."

"Dear Inspector, poor Spitaleri can't do it any differently, otherwise he'd be operating at a loss."

"Anything else?"

Fazio made a vague expression.

"Rumors."

"Meaning?"

"He likes minors. A lot."

"A pedophile?"

"Chief, I don't know what you call it, but the fact is, he likes young girls around fourteen, fifteen years old."

"But not sixteen?"

"No, he thinks they're past their prime."

"He must be one of those who often goes abroad: a 'sex tourist.'"

"Yessir, but he finds 'em here, too. And he's not wanting for money. In town they say that one time a girl's mother and father wanted to report him, but he paid out millions of lire and dodged the bullet. Another time, when he deflowered a virgin, he paid for it with an apartment."

"And does he find people willing to sell him their daughters?"

"Chief, don't we live in a free-market economy these days? And isn't the free market the sign of democracy, liberty, and progress?"

Montalbano gawked at him, open-mouthed.

"Why are you looking at me like that?"

"Because you just said something I should have said . . ."

The telephone rang.

"Chief, there's a Signor Spitaletti here says he gots—"

"Yes, send him in." He turned to Fazio: "Did you tell him why he was summoned?"

"What, are you kidding? Of course not."

Spitaleri, tanned to the point of being brown, finely dressed in a green jacket as light as onionskin and sporting a Rolex, shoulder-length hair, a gold bracelet, a gold crucifix one could barely see amidst the chest hair sticking out of his unbuttoned shirt, and yellow moccasin loafers and no socks, was visibly nervous about being called in. The way he sat on the edge of the chair said it all. He spoke first.

"I came, just as you asked, but, believe me, I have no idea—"

"You will."

Why did the guy provoke such a violent aversion in him? He decided to put on the usual act to waste time.

"Fazio, have you finished over there with Franceschini?"

There was no Franceschini over there, but Fazio had a lot of experience playing the straight man.

"Not yet, sir."

"Listen, I'll be right over, that way we can finish this business in five minutes."

Turning towards Spitaleri, he stood up.

"Just sit tight a minute, then I'm all yours."

"Look, Inspector, I have an engagement that—"

"I understand."

They went into Fazio's office.

"Ask Catarella to make me a coffee with my pot. You want some?"

"No thanks, Chief."

He took his time sipping his coffee, then went out to the parking lot to smoke a cigarette. Spitaleri had arrived in a black Ferrari. Which increased the inspector's dislike for the developer. Having a Ferrari in a small town was like keeping a lion in the bathroom of your apartment.

When he returned to his office with Fazio, they found Spitaleri with his cell phone to his ear and talking.

"... to Filiberto. Listen, I'll get back to you later," said Spitaleri, seeing them enter. He put his cell phone back in his pocket.

"I see you were calling from here," Montalbano severely, beginning an improvisation worthy of the commedia dell'arte.

"Why? Am I not allowed?" Spitaleri asked belligerently.

"You should have told me."

Spitaleri turned red with rage.

"I don't have to tell you anything! Until proven to the contrary, I am a free citizen! If you have something to—"

"Calm down, Mr. Spitaleri. You're making a big mistake."

"No, there's no mistake! You're treating me like someone under arrest!"

"Under arrest? Who ever said anything about arrest?"

"I want my lawyer!"

"Mr. Spitaleri, please listen to what I have to tell you, then you can decide whether or not to call your lawyer."

"All right, speak."

"Now, then. If you had told me you wanted to phone someone, I would have dutifully informed you that all calls into and out of every police station in Italy, even those made with cell phones, are intercepted and recorded."

"What?!"

"Oh, yes. You heard right. A recent directive of the Ministry of the Interior. You know, with all the terrorism . . ."

Spitaleri had turned pale as a corpse.

"I want that tape!"

"You always want something! Your lawyer, the tape . . ."

Fazio, the foil, started laughing.

"Ha-ha-ha! He wants the tape!"

"Yes, I do. And I don't see what's so funny about that!"

"Let me explain," Montalbano interjected. "We don't have any tapes here. The conversations are intercepted directly by the anti-Mafia and antiterrorism commissions in Rome via satellite. And they are recorded there. To avoid all interference, deletion, omissions. Understand?"

Spitaleri was sweating so profusely he looked like a geyser.

"Then what happens?"

"If, when listening to the intercepted conversation, they hear anything suspicious, they inform us from Rome, and we begin investigating. Excuse me, but you, what reason do you have to be worried? You don't have a record, you're not a terrorist, you're not in the Mafia—"

"Of course, but . . ."

"But?"

"You see . . . about three weeks ago, at one of my work-sites in Montelusa, there was an accident."

Montalbano glanced at Fazio, who signaled to him that he knew nothing about it.

"What sort of accident?"

"A worker . . . an Arab . . ."

"An illegal immigrant?"

"Apparently, yes . . . But I had been assured—"

"—that he was legal."

"Yes. Because he was in the process—"

"—of being legalized."

"So you know everything!"

"Precisely."

6

And, flashing a sly smile, he added:

"We know all about that case."

"Do we ever know about it!" Fazio laid it on even thicker, again laughing abrasively.

The lie was as big as a house.

"He fell from the scaffolding—" the inspector ventured.

"—on the third floor," said Spitaleri, now drenched in sweat. "It happened, as you probably know, on a Saturday. When there was no sign of him at the end of the day, everybody thought he'd already left. We didn't find out until Monday, when work resumed at the construction site."

"Yeah, I know, that's what we were told by—"

"—Inspector Lozupone of Montelusa, who conducted a very serious investigation," Spitaleri concluded.

"Right, Lozupone. By the way, what was the Arab's name again? I can't quite remember."

"I can't remember, either."

Montalbano thought they ought to build a great big monument, like the Vittoriano in Rome for the Unknown Soldier, to commemorate all the illegal immigrants who have died on the job for a crust of bread.

"Well, but, you know, that business about the protective railing . . ."

A second shot in the dark.

"Oh, there was a protective railing, Inspector, I swear to God there was! Your colleague saw it with his own two eyes. The truth of the matter is that that Arab was totally drunk, climbed over the railing, and fell."

"Are you aware of the autopsy results?"

"Me? No."

"No trace of alcohol was found in the blood."

Another whopper. Montalbano was firing blindly away.

"But on his clothing there sure was!" said Fazio, with the usual laugh.

He, too, was shooting blindly, come what may.

Spitaleri said nothing. He didn't even feign surprise.

"Who were you talking to just now?" the inspector asked, going back to square one.

"With the yard foreman."

"And what did you say to him? You don't have to answer, of course, but it's in your own best interests . . ."

"First I told him that I was sure you had summoned me here to ask me about this business of the Arab, and then—"

"That's enough, Signor Spitaleri, say no more," said the inspector in a magnanimous tone. "I am required to respect your privacy, you know. And I do so not out of formal observance of the law, but out of a deep sense of respect for others, which is something I was born with. If Rome tells me anything, I'll call you back here for questioning."

Behind the developer's back, Fazio mimed the gesture

of clapping his hands, applauding Montalbano's performance.

"So I can go?"

"No."

"Why not?"

"Well, you see, I didn't summon you here concerning the investigation into your employee's death, but for something else entirely. Do you remember if it was you who designed and built a house in the Pizzo district at Marina di Montereale?"

"For Angelo Speciale? Yes."

"It is my duty to inform you that a crime was committed. We discovered some illegal construction, an entire underground level."

Spitaleri could not repress a sigh of relief. Then he started laughing. Had he expected a more serious charge?

"So, you found it! Well, you're wasting your time. That's pure chickenshit, if you'll excuse my language! Look, Inspector, around here you're practically required to engage in illegal construction just to avoid looking like an idiot in other people's eyes! Everybody does it! All that needs to be done is for Speciale to request amnesty, and—"

"That doesn't change the fact that you, as builder and works superintendent, didn't abide by the terms of the building permit."

"But, Inspector, I repeat, that's all bullshit!"

"It's a crime."

"A crime, you say? I would call it a minor mistake, the

kind that used to get marked in red pencil. Believe me, you would do better not to report me."

"Are you threatening me, by any chance?"

"I would never do that in the presence of a witness. It's just that, if you report me, you'll be the laughingstock of the whole town. You'll look like a fool."

He was getting bold, the motherfucking crook. Over that business about the phone call, he was practically shitting his pants, whereas illegal construction only made him laugh.

So Montalbano decided to shoot him straight in the face.

"Maybe you're right. Unfortunately, however, I still have to look into that illegal apartment."

"But, why, can you tell me?"

"Because we found a dead body inside."

"A dead . . . body?"

"Yes, of a fifteen-year-old girl. A minor. Little more than a child. With her throat slashed. A horror."

He purposely stressed the words referring to the victim's tender age.

And, in fact, Spitaleri suddenly extended his arms, as if trying to fend off a force that was pushing him backwards, then he tried to stand up, but his legs and breath failed him, and he fell back into the chair.

"Water!" he managed with difficulty to articulate.

They gave him the water, and they sent for a cognac from the bar on the corner.

"Feel better?"

Spitaleri, who still didn't seem in any condition to speak, gestured with his hand that he felt so-so.

"Listen, Mr. Spitaleri, for now I'll do the talking, and you can shake your head yes or no. Okay?"

The developer nodded.

"The little girl's murder can only have happened on the day before or the day itself when the illegal floor was buried. If it happened the day before, then the killer hid the body somewhere and didn't bring it inside until the next day—and just in the nick of time, since the underground floor became inaccessible after that point. You follow?"

Another nod.

"If, on the other hand, the murder took place on the last day, the killer must have left a small opening, pushed the girl in, then, once inside, raped her, slit her throat, and stuck her into the trunk. After which he left the apartment and closed up the only remaining opening. Do you agree?"

Spitaleri threw his hands up, as if to say he didn't know what to say.

"Did you oversee the work up until the last day?"

The developer shook his head.

"Why not?"

Spitaleri spread his arms and made a rumbling sound.

"Rrrrrrhhhhhhhh . . ."

Was he imitating an airplane?

"You were flying?"

Another nod.

"How many masons were used to bury the illegal apartment?"

Spitaleri held up two fingers.

Was this any way to carry on an investigation? It was starting to look like a comedy routine.

"Mr. Spitaleri, I'm getting tired of seeing you answer in this fashion. Among other things, I'm beginning to wonder if you think we're a bunch of dumbasses that you can fuck around with." He turned to Fazio. "Were you wondering the same thing?"

"Yeah, I was."

"So, you know what you're gonna do? You're gonna take him into the bathroom, make him strip down naked, then give him a cold shower until he recovers his senses."

"I want my lawyer!" yelled Spitaleri, miraculously recovering his voice.

"You think it's such a good idea to publicize this?"

"What do you mean?"

"I mean that, if you call your lawyer, I'll call the newsmen. I believe I remember you have a history in matters of young girls ... If those guys turn it into a public trial, you're fucked. If, on the other hand, you cooperate, you can walk out of here in five minutes."

Pale as a corpse, the developer was overcome by a sudden fit of the shakes.

"What else do you want to know?"

"Just now you said you hadn't been able to see the work through to the end, because you'd taken a plane somewhere. How many days before?"

"I left on the morning of the last day of work."

"And do you remember the date of this last day?"

"The twelfth of October."

Fazio and Montalbano exchanged glances.

"So you're in a position to tell me whether, in the living room, aside from the fixtures wrapped in plastic, there was also a trunk."

"There was."

"Are you sure about that?"

"Absolutely. And it was empty. Mr. Speciale himself had us carry it down there. He'd used it to bring some stuff from Germany. And since it was half broken and had become almost unusable, he had it put in the living room downstairs instead of throwing it away. He said he might need it later on."

"Tell me the names of the two masons who were the last to work on the house."

"I don't remember."

"Then you'd better call your lawyer," said Montalbano. "Because I'm going to accuse you of being an accessory to—"

"But I really don't remember!"

"I'm sorry for you, but—"

"Can I make a call to Dipasquale?"

"Who's he?"

"A foreman."

"The same one you called earlier?"

"Yes. That's him, Dipasquale. He was the foreman when we built Speciale's house."

"Go ahead and call, but remember: Don't say anything that might compromise you. Don't forget about the phone taps."

Spitaleri dug out his cell phone and dialed a number.

"Hello, 'Ngilino? 'Ss me. Do you by any chance remember the names of the masons who worked for us six years ago, on the construction of the house at Pizzo, in Marina di Montereale? No? So what am I supposed to do? It's Inspector Montalbano who wants to know. Oh, yes, that's true, you're right. Sorry."

"Listen, before I forget, would you give me Angelo Dipasquale's cell phone number? Fazio, write it down."

Spitaleri dictated it to him.

"So?" Montalbano pressed him.

"Dipasquale can't remember the names of the masons. But they're definitely in my office somewhere. Can I go get them?"

"Go right ahead."

The developer stood up and nearly ran to the door.

"Wait a minute. Fazio's going with you and will bring the names and addresses back to me. You, meanwhile, have to remain available."

"What does that mean?"

"It means you are not to leave the Vigàta area. If you need to go anywhere farther away, you must let me know. Speaking of which, do you remember where you were flying to on the twelfth of October?"

"I . . . to Bangkok."

"You really like fresh meat, eh?"

The moment Spitaleri and Fazio went out, Montalbano phoned Spitaleri's foreman. He didn't want to give the developer time to talk to him and get their stories straight.

"Dipasquale? Inspector Montalbano here. How long would it take you to come down to the Vigàta police station from your worksite?"

"Half an hour, at the most. But it's no use asking me, 'cause I can't come now. I'm working."

"I'm working, too. And my work involves telling you to come here now."

"I repeat, I can't."

"What do you say I send somebody to get you in one of our cars with sirens blaring, right in front of all your men?"

"But what do you want from me?"

"Just come, and I'll satisfy your curiosity. You've got twenty-five minutes."

It took him twenty-two minutes flat to get there. To save time, he hadn't even changed clothes. He was still in his lime-stained overalls. Dipasquale was about fifty, with hair entirely white but a black moustache. Short and stocky, he never looked at the person he was speaking to, and when he did, he had a troubled gaze.

"I don't understand why first you called Mr. Spitaleri about that Arab, and then you called me about the house at Pizzo."

"I didn't call you about the house at Pizzo."

"Oh, no? Why'd you call me, then?"

"About the death of that Arab mason. What was his name?"

"I don't remember. But it was an accident! The guy was completely drunk! Those people start drinking first thing in the morning, every day! Never mind Saturday! In fact, Inspector Lupuzone concluded that—"

"Forget about my colleague's conclusions. Tell me exactly what happened."

"But I already told the judge and the inspector—"

"The third time's a charm."

"Oh, all right. At five-thirty that Saturday, we finished working and went home. Then, on Monday morning—"

"Stop right there. Didn't you notice that the Arab wasn't there?"

"No. What am I supposed to do, take roll call?"

"Who closes up the worksite?"

"The watchman. Filiberto. Filiberto Attanasio."

But when they came in and caught Spitaleri talking on the phone, hadn't he said that very name, Filiberto?

"Why do you need a watchman? Don't you pay for protection?"

"There's always some young drug addict that might—"

"I see. Where can I find him?"

"Filiberto? He's also the watchman at the site we're working at now. In fact, he sleeps there."

"In the open air?"

"No, there's a prefab made out of corrugated tin."

"Tell me the exact location of this construction site."

Dipasquale told him.

"Go on."

"But I've already told you everything I know! We found him dead on Monday morning. He fell from the scaffolding on the third floor. He'd climbed over the protective railing, drunk as a skunk. It was an accident, I tell you!"

"For now, we'll stop here."

"So I can go now?"

"In just a minute. Were you there when the work was completed?"

Dipasquale balked.

"But the construction in Montelusa's still not finished!"

"I'm talking about the house at Pizzo."

"But didn't you say you called me in to talk about the Arab?"

"I just changed my mind. Is that all right with you?"

"Do I have any choice?"

"You know, of course, that a whole floor was built illegally at Pizzo?"

Dipasquale looked neither surprised nor concerned.

"Of course I know. But I was just following orders."

"Do you know what the word 'accomplice' means?"

"Yeah, I know."

"Then tell me."

"Well, there's accomplice and accomplice. To call helping somebody build an illegal floor on a house an accomplice is like calling a pinprick a fatal injury."

He even knew how to debate, did the foreman.

"Did you stay at Pizzo until the work was completed?"

"No, Mr. Spitaleri transferred me to Fela four days before, 'cause they were just finishing setting up another construction site there. But everything was just about done at Pizzo. We only had to seal off the illegal floor and cover it up with sand. That was easy work, there wasn't no need of supervisors. I remember I hired two masons, but I forget their names. Like I said to Spitaleri, you can find those names by looking—"

"Yes, Spitaleri went to look for them. Listen, do you know if Mr. Speciale stayed until the work was finished?"

"He was there as long as I was there. And that crazy stepson of his was there, too, that German kid."

"Why did you call him crazy?"

"Because he was."

"What did he do that was so unusual?"

"He could stand on 'is head for an hour straight with his feet in the air. An' he used to get down on all fours and eat grass like a sheep."

"Is that all?"

"When nature called, he would drop his pants and do it right in front of everybody without feeling embarrassed."

"But nowadays there are a lot of people like him, no? They call themselves nature-lovers, with good reason, I guess . . . All things considered, it doesn't seem to me like this German was so crazy."

"Wait. One day he went down to the beach, it was summertime and there were people there, and he got it in his head to strip down bare-naked and start chasing a girl wit' 'is dick hanging out and all."

"So what happened?"

"It turned out a couple of young guys who was there grabbed him and busted his head."

Maybe Ralf had got it in his head to pretend he was Mallarmé's faun. But what the foreman was saying was very interesting.

"Do you know of any other episodes like this one?"

"Yes. They told me he did the same thing with another young girl he met on the path that leads from the provincial road to Pizzo."

"What did he do?"

"Soon as he saw her, he took off all his clothes and started chasing her."

"And how did the girl get away?"

"Well, just then Mr. Spitaleri drove by in his car."

Just the right man at the right moment! A whole slew of clichés came into Montalbano's head: from the frying pan into the fire, between a rock and a hard place ... He felt irked at himself for having such obvious thoughts.

"Listen, I suppose Mr. Speciale knew about his stepson's exploits?"

"Oh, yeah!"

"And what did he say about it?"

"Nothing. He would start laughing. He said the kid had his moments in Germany, too, but was harmless. All he wanted to do to the girls was kiss 'em, that's what Mr. Speciale told us. But what I want to know is this: Why'd the blessed kid need to take off all his clothes if all he wanted to do is kiss the girls?"

"All right, you can go now. But make yourself available to us."

Dipasquale had spontaneously offered him Ralf's head on a platter not silver but gold. Especially since the foreman, thus far, knew nothing about the murdered girl he'd found. So Montalbano had an embarrassment of riches to choose from, as far as sex maniacs went: Spitaleri and Ralf. There were just two little problems. The young German had disappeared on his way back to Germany, and on that terrible twelfth of October, Spitaleri was traveling.

7

Just to kill some time while waiting for Fazio to return, he decided to phone Forensics.

"I'd like to speak to Dr. Arquà. Montalbano here."

"Please hold."

He had enough time for a leisurely review of the multiplication tables of six, seven, eight, and nine.

"Inspector Montalbano? I'm sorry, but Dr. Arquà is engaged at the moment."

"And when will he be disengaged?"

"Please call back in about ten minutes."

Engaged? Right, to be married to his dog. The fucking asshole was playing hard to get. Getting precious. But how precious could an asshole get? And can an asshole increase in value?

He got up, left the room and, when passing by Catarella, said:

"I'm gonna go have a coffee at the port. I'll be right back."

Once outside, he realized there was no way. In the parking lot the heat was similar to what one feels when standing in front of a blazing fireplace. He touched the handle on the car door and burned himself. Cursing the saints, he went back inside. Catarella looked bewildered and glanced at his watch. He couldn't figure out how the inspector had managed to go to the port, drink a coffee, and come back in such a short time.

"Catarella, go make me a cup of coffee."

"Anutter one, Chief? Din't you juss have one? 'Ss not good to drink too much coffee."

"You're right. Forget about it."

"I'd like to speak with Dr. Arquà, if he's been disengaged, that is. Montalbano here, same as before."

"Please hold."

No multiplication tables this time, but a few laborious attempts at singing a tune that must have been by the Rolling Stones, then another that was probably by the Beatles but came out almost the same as the first because he didn't exactly have perfect pitch.

"Inspector Montalbano? Dr. Arquà is still engaged. If you want, try calling back—"

"—in about ten minutes, I know, I know."

But why was he wasting all this time on an imbecile who was surely enjoying making him wait? He rolled up two sheets of paper into a ball and stuck it in his mouth. Then he pinched his nostrils shut with a binder clip and redialed the forensic lab's number. He spoke with a slight Tuscan accent.

"This is Plenipotentiary Minister and Supervisor General Gianfilippo Maradona. Please get me Dr. Arquà at once."

"Right away, your excellency."

Montalbano spit out the ball of paper and removed the clamp. Half a minute later, Arquà came on the line.

"Good day, your excellency, what can I do for you?"

"Excuse me, why are you calling me 'your excellency'? This is Montalbano."

"But I was told that—"

"But you can keep calling me that, I rather like it."

Arquà let a few moments of silence pass. It was clear he was tempted to hang up, but then he made up his mind.

"What do you want?"

"Do you have anything to tell me?"

"Yes."

"Then tell me."

"You're supposed to say 'please.' "

"Please."

"Question."

"Where was she killed?"

"Where she was found."

"In the exact same place?"

"Next to what would have been the French door in the living room."

"Are you sure about that?"

"Absolutely."

"Why?"

"Because a pool of blood had formed there."

"Anywhere else?"

"No, nothing."

"Just that pool?"

"There were streaks from her being dragged from the pool over to a spot next to the trunk."

"Did you find the weapon?"

"No."

"Fingerprints?"

"A billion."

"Even on the plastic wrapped around the body?"

"No, nothing there."

"Find anything else?"

"The roll of packing tape. The same that was used for the fixtures."

"No fingerprints there, either?"

"Nothing."

"Is that all?"

"That's all."

"Fuck you."

"Same to you."

Nice exchange. Terse and crisp as a dialogue from one of Vittorio Alfieri's tragedies.

One thing, however, had come out: that the killing had to have taken place on the masons' last day of work.

He couldn't stay in his office any longer. His brain felt reduced to a kind of dense marmalade in which his thoughts had trouble circulating and sometimes got stuck.

Was a chief inspector allowed to go bare-chested in his

own office? Was there any rule prohibiting this? No, one needed only hope that no outsider came in unannounced.

He got up and closed the shutter to the window, through which no air was passing, only heat. He half-shut the inside blinds, turned on the light, and removed his shirt.

"Catarella!"

"Coming!"

When Catarella saw him, he said:

"Lucky youse that can do it!"

"Listen, don't let anyone in without telling me first. I mean it. And another thing—call some store that sells fans and have a rather big one delivered here."

Since there was still no sign of Fazio, he dialed another number.

"Dr. Pasquano? Montalbano here."

"Would you believe it? I was just now regretting that no one was breaking my balls."

"See? I sensed it and took immediate action."

"What the fuck do you want?"

The usual refined, aristocratic courtesy from Pasquano.

"Don't you know?"

"I'm going to work on that girl this afternoon. Call me tomorrow morning."

"Not tonight?"

"Tonight I'm going to the club. I've got a serious poker game to attend, and I don't want any—"

"I understand. So you didn't give the body even a superficial glance?"

"Very superficial."

From the way he said it, the inspector gathered that the
doctor had arrived at some sort of conclusion. The problem
was handling him the right way.

"You're going to the club around nine, right?"

"Yes. Why?"

"Because around ten I'm going to show up at the club
with a couple of uniformed men and raise such a stink that
I'll fuck up your poker game."

Montalbano heard him chuckle.

"So, what do you say?"

"I can confirm that she wasn't more than sixteen
years old."

"And?"

"The killer slit her throat."

"With what?"

"With one of those knives you carry around in your
pocket, but which are sharp as razors. Like the Opinel brand."

"Could you tell if he was left-handed?"

"Yes, if I look into a crystal ball."

"Is that so hard to establish?"

"Hard enough. And I don't feel like bullshitting."

"I do it all the time! Let me have the satisfaction of hearing you bullshit just once."

"Look, it's just a hypothesis, mind you, but in my opinion the murderer was not left-handed."

"On what do you base that statement?"

"I got a certain sense of the position."

"What position?"

"Haven't you ever happened to leaf through the *Kama Sutra*?"

"Explain what you mean."

"Look, let me repeat my disclaimer that this is just a theory. The man persuades the girl to follow him into a part of the house that is now almost entirely covered in dirt. Once he's got her inside, he has only two thoughts in his head. The first is to fuck her, the second is to find the right moment to kill her."

"So you think it was premeditated murder, not temporary insanity or something similar?"

"I'm merely explaining my own conjecture."

"But why did he want to kill her?"

"Maybe they'd had prior relations, and the girl had asked him for a lot of money to keep quiet. You have to bear in mind that she was a minor, and it's quite possible the man was married. Don't you think that's a good motive?"

"Yes, in fact."

"Can I go on?"

"Of course."

"The man has her take all her clothes off, he does the same, and then has her bend down in front of him, bracing herself with her hands against the wall, as he fucks her from behind. When the time is right—"

"Will the autopsy be able to establish if there were sexual relations?"

"Six years later? Are you crazy? Anyway, I was saying, when the time is right—"

"What's that supposed to mean?"

"As the girl is reaching orgasm and is therefore not in a position to react promptly."

"Go on."

"He grabs the knife."

"Stop. Where does he grab it from, if he's naked?"

"How the fuck should I know where he gets it from! Look, if you keep interrupting me, I'm going to change the story and tell you about Snow White and the Seven Dwarfs instead."

"Sorry. Please continue."

"He grabs the knife—you can figure out yourself where from—and cuts her throat and, shoving her forward, he jumps backwards. He waits for her to bleed to death, then spreads a big sheet of plastic across the floor. After all, there are so many lying about—"

"Wait a second. Before grabbing the sheet of plastic, he puts on latex gloves."

"Why?"

"Because there are no fingerprints on that plastic. Arquà told me. Nor on the adhesive tape."

"You see? It was all premeditated. He even had the gloves in his pocket! Shall I go on?"

"Yes."

"He wraps up the body and puts it in the trunk. When he's finished, he gets dressed. He probably hasn't got a single drop of blood on his clothes."

"What about the girl's clothes, underwear and shoes?"

"Nowadays girls go around very lightly dressed. All the man would have needed was a plastic bag to make off with it all."

"Okay, but why did he make off with it instead of putting it inside the trunk?"

"I don't know. It could have been an irrational move. Murderers don't always behave rationally. You know that better than I do. Is that enough for you?"

"Yes and no."

"Or else he might be a fetishist who every now and then pulls out the girl's clothes, sniffs them to smell her scent, and jacks himself off to his heart's content."

"But how did you arrive at this conclusion?"

"About the jacking off, you mean?"

Pasquano was in a playful mood.

"I was referring to your reconstruction of the murder."

"Oh, that? By looking closely at how and where the tip of the knife went in, and by considering the line of the cut. Among other things, the girl kept her head down, with her chin touching her chest, and this helped me figure out the way things went, given the fact that the murderer also slashed her right cheek as he was pulling the knife out of her throat."

"Any distinguishing marks?"

"For identification? She had an appendectomy scar and a rare congenital malformation on her right foot."

"Namely?"

"Varus in the big toe."

"In plain words?"

"It was bent inwards."

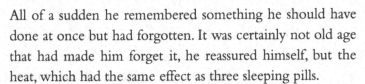

All of a sudden he remembered something he should have done at once but had forgotten. It was certainly not old age that had made him forget it, he reassured himself, but the heat, which had the same effect as three sleeping pills.

"Catarella? Come into my office."

He materialized a quarter of a second later.

"Your orders, sir."

"I need you to do a search on the computer."

" 'Ats what I'm here for, Chief."

"You must see if you can find if anyone ever reported the disappearance of a sixteen-year-old girl. If so, it would have been around the thirteenth or fourteenth of October 1999."

"I'll get on it straightaways."

"And what about that fan?"

"Chief, I called four diffrint shops. The fans're all sold out. One guy told me alls he had was balls."

"What kind of balls?"

"The kind you attach to the ceiling. I'll go try a few other stores."

The inspector waited half an hour, and since there was still no sign of Fazio, he went out to eat. Merely getting into his car and driving the short stretch of road to the trattoria was enough to drench his shirt by the time he arrived.

"Inspector," said Enzo, "it's too hot to eat hot food."

"So what have you got?"

"How about a few big platters of *antipasto di mare* with shrimp, prawns, baby octopus, anchovies, sardines, mussels, and clams?"

"Sounds good. And for the second course?"

"Mullet in onions: served cold, they're a delight. Then, at the end, to cleanse the palate, my wife made some lemon sorbet."

Either because of the heat or because of his stomach, which felt very heavy, he skipped his customary walk along the jetty and went straight home.

Opening all the windows and doors in the vain hope of creating even the slightest of drafts, he lay down naked in bed, on top of the sheets, for an hour's nap. Then, when he awoke, he put on his bathing suit and went for a swim, risking heart failure.

He cooled himself off nicely and, once back in the house, felt like hearing Livia's voice.

What to do? He decided to set aside his pride and call her.

"Oh, it's you?" said Livia, sounding neither surprised nor glad.

Actually—let's admit it—she was downright antarctic.

"How was the drive back?"

"Horrendous. Hot as hell. The car's air-conditioning

broke. Then, when we stopped at an Autogrill after Grosseto, Bruno disappeared."

"The kid has a gift for it."

"Please, don't start in with your wisecracks."

"I was merely stating a fact. Where did he end up?"

"We lost two hours looking for him. He'd gone and hidden himself inside the cab of a tractor-trailer."

"What about the driver?"

"He hadn't noticed a thing. He was sleeping. Well, I have to go."

"Where are you going?"

"My cousin Massimiliano is waiting for me downstairs. You caught me purely by chance; I'd come up to get some clothes."

"Where have you been?"

"With Guido and Laura, at their villa."

"And now you're leaving?"

"Yes, with Massimiliano. We're going on a little cruise with his boat."

"How many of you are there?"

"Just him and me. Bye."

"Bye."

And where the hell did her dear cousin Massimiliano find the money to maintain a cruiser, considering that he didn't work and spent his days counting flies? Montalbano would have done better not to call.

He was about to leave the house when the telephone rang.

"Hello?"

"Most of all, you're a man who doesn't keep his word!"

It was Livia, apparently spoiling for a fight.

"Me?!"

"Yes, you!"

"Mind telling me when I didn't keep my word?"

"You swore to me that there were no murders in Vigàta during the summer."

"How can you make such a statement! I swore? At the most, I probably said that with the summer heat, anyone planning on killing somebody would decide to postpone it till autumn."

"So how is it that Guido and Laura ended up sharing their bed with a murder victim in the middle of August?"

"Livia, stop exaggerating! Sharing their bed!"

"Well, practically."

"Listen carefully. That murder dates from the month of October, six years ago. October, did you get that? Which means, among other things, that my theory was not just hot air."

"What matters to me is that, all because of you—"

"All because of me?! If that little imp Bruno hadn't given in to the temptation to emulate Houdini—"

"Houdi who?"

"Houdini, a famous magician. If Bruno hadn't gone and disappeared underground, nobody would have known there was a corpse downstairs, and your friends could have gone right on sleeping soundly."

"Your cynicism is repugnant."

She hung up.

When he got back to the station, it was almost six o'clock.

He had wanted to go earlier, but when he stepped outside the door to his house, he was assailed by a blast of heat so intense that he went back inside. Taking his clothes off, he filled the tub with cold water and lay in it for an hour.

"Ahhh, Chief, Chief! I found 'er. I idinnificated the girl!"

Arms extended away from his body, fingers stretched and spread out, he was strutting like a peacock.

"Come into my office."

Catarella followed him with a sheet of paper in hand and an attitude so exultant that one could almost hear, in the background, the triumphal march from *Aïda*.

8

Montalbano glanced at the file that Catarella had printed out for him.

> MORREALE, Caterina, known as "Rina"
> daughter of Giuseppe Morreale and Francesca Dibetta
> born in Vigàta July 3, 1983
> residing in Vigàta, at via Roma 42
> disappeared October 12, 1999
> reported missing by father on October 13, 1999
> Height: 5 ft. 9 in.
> Hair: blond
> Eyes: blue
> Build: slender
> Distinguishing marks: small scar from appendectomy and
>   varus of right big toe
>
> NOTE: Bulletin issued by Fiacca Central Police

He pushed away the sheet of paper, buried his face in his hands.

Throat slashed worse than if she'd been a sheep, or any kind of animal at all.

Now that he'd seen, from the accompanying photo, what she looked like, he felt sure, for no apparent reason, that Dr. Pasquano was simultaneously right and wrong.

He was right about how she'd been killed, but wrong about why she'd been killed. Pasquano had advanced the hypothesis of blackmail, but Rina Morreale, with her serene blue eyes, would never have been capable of blackmail.

Even if she had consented to making love with the man who would later kill her, how could she ever have followed him underground of her own accord, into an illegal apartment that one entered through a narrow, even dangerous opening? Above all, it must have been pitch-dark down there. Had the murderer perhaps brought a flashlight with him?

But wasn't there a better place? Couldn't they have done it in a car? Pizzo was a secluded spot; it wouldn't have been a problem.

No, Rina Morreale was definitely forced by the killer to enter what would become her tomb.

Catarella had come up beside him to look at the photograph of the girl. Maybe he hadn't paid much attention to it before.

"She was so beautyfull!" he said softly, moved.

The photo was consistent with the description and showed a girl of rare beauty. Her neck looked like it could have been painted by Botticelli.

There was no need to do any more searches. He had

only to inform the family so that somebody could go to Montelusa to identify the body.

Montalbano felt his heart ache.

"She was so beautyfull!" Catarella repeated in a low voice.

Looking up, the inspector caught him turned three-quarters away, drying his eyes with the sleeve of his jacket.

Better change the subject at once.

"Is Fazio back?"

"Yessir."

"Could you go call him for me?"

Fazio, too, had a sheet of paper in his hand when he came in.

"Catarella told me the girl's been identified. Can I see her?"

Montalbano handed him the printout. Fazio looked at it, then gave it back to him.

"Poor kid."

"When we catch him—because we will catch him, of that much I am certain—I'm going to smash his face in," the inspector said quietly.

A thought had just come to him.

"How is it," he continued, "that the girl's parents reported her missing to the Fiacca police?"

"I don't understand it, Chief, even though it happened during the period of cooperation between all the different commissariats regardless of territorial boundaries. Remember all the confusion?"

"How could I forget? Since we had to deal with everything, we couldn't deal with anything. Anyway, let's not forget to ask the parents."

"Speaking of which, who's going to tell them?"

"You are. But inform Tommaseo first. In fact, do it right now, from this phone. That way we won't have to think about it anymore."

Fazio spoke with the prosecutor, who wanted the file sent to him by e-mail. But before alerting the parents, the inspector wanted to talk with Pasquano and be absolutely certain of the identification.

"Catarella!"

"Here I am, Chief."

"Take the girl's file and send it immediately to Prosecutor Tommaseo."

After Catarella took it away, Montalbano went on the attack.

"How did it take you all morning to find those names?"

"It wasn't my job to find them, Chief, it was Spitaleri's."

"But haven't they got a computer or some other sort of filing system?"

"They have, but they keep only the information from the last five years in the office, and since that house was built six years ago . . ."

"And where do they keep the rest of it?"

"At the house of Spitaleri's sister, who, it turns out, went to Montelusa this morning, so we had to wait till she got back."

"I don't understand why he keeps these documents at his sister's house."

"I do."

"Then tell me."

"Because of the Finance Police. In the event of an unannounced visit by the auditors. That way, Spitaleri has time to forewarn his sister. Who has been instructed beforehand and knows which documents to bring and which not to bring to the office. Does that explain it?"

"Perfectly."

"Anyway, the masons who were working—" Fazio began.

"Wait a minute. We still haven't had a chance to talk about Spitaleri."

"Concerning the girl's murder—"

"No. For now I want to talk about Spitaleri the real estate developer. Not the Spitaleri who likes underage girls. We can talk about him afterwards. What did you make of him?"

"Chief, the guy smells fishy to me. When we made up the story about the autopsy not finding any alcohol in the Arab's blood but only on his clothes, he didn't react. Not a peep. Whereas he should have either been surprised or said it couldn't be true."

"Therefore they must have drenched the poor bastard in wine after he died, so people would think he was drunk."

"So what do you think happened, Chief?"

"When you were out with Spitaleri, I called in the foreman, Dipasquale, and interrogated him. In my opinion, the Arab fell off the unprotected scaffolding and none of his comrades noticed. Maybe he was working alone in some concealed area of the structure. Then the worksite's watchman, whose name is Filiberto Attanasio, finds the body after everybody's gone home and calls up Dipasquale, who informs Spitaleri in turn. What's wrong? Are you listening to me?"

Fazio looked lost in thought.

"What did you say the watchman's name was?"

"Filiberto Attanasio."

"Would you excuse me for a minute?"

He got up, went out, and returned five minutes later with a printout in hand.

"I remember him well," he said.

He handed Montalbano the printout. Filiberto Attanasio had been convicted several times for larceny, aggravated assault, attempted homicide, and armed robbery. The photo showed a fiftyish man with an oversized nose and nary a hair on his head. He was classified as an habitual offender.

"A good thing to know" was the inspector's comment. Then he said, "After being informed by the watchman, they check out the situation and decide to cover their asses by putting up a protective railing, which they hadn't already done, at the crack of dawn on Sunday. They drench the body in wine and go home to sleep. The following morning, thanks to the watchman, they work it all out."

"And Inspector Lozupone swallows it."

"You think so? Do you know Lozupone?"

"No. But I certainly know who he is."

"I've known him a long time. He's not—"

The phone rang.

"Chief? 'At'd be Proxeter Dommaseo onna phone wanting a talk to you poissonally in poisson."

"Put him on."

"Montalbano? Tommaseo."

"Tommaseo? Montalbano."

The prosecutor got disoriented.

"I wanted to tell you ... er ... ah, yes, I've seen the photo on the printout. What a beautiful girl!"

"Right."

"Raped and slaughtered!"

"Did Dr. Pasquano tell you she'd been raped?"

"No, he told me only she'd had her throat slashed. But I sense intuitively that she was raped. In fact, I'm sure of it."

As if the public prosecutor's brain wouldn't be working round the clock trying to imagine the crime scene down to the finest detail!

At this moment, Montalbano had a truly brilliant idea that might perhaps spare him or Fazio the unpleasant task of breaking the tragic news to the girl's family.

"You know something, Tommaseo? Apparently the girl has a twin sister, or so I've been told, who is far more beautiful than the victim."

"More beautiful? Really?"

"Apparently, yes,"

"So today this twin sister would be twenty-two years old."

"It adds up."

Fazio was glaring at him, dumbfounded. What on earth was the inspector concocting?

There was a pause. Surely the prosecutor, his eyes glued to the photo in the dossier, was licking his chops at the thought of meeting the twin sister. Then he spoke.

"You know what, Montalbano? I think it's better if I go in person to inform the family . . . given the victim's tender age . . . and the particularly savage manner . . ."

"You're absolutely right, sir. You are a man of profound human understanding. So you'll take care of telling the family?"

"Yes. It seems only right."

They said good-bye and hung up. Fazio, having understood the inspector's game, started laughing.

"Man, that guy, the minute he hears talk of a woman . . ."

"Forget about him. He'll dash over to the Morreales' house hoping to meet a twin sister who doesn't exist. What was I saying to you before he called?"

"You were telling me about Inspector Lozupone."

"Ah, yes. Lozupone's been around, he's smart, and he knows what's what."

"What's that supposed to mean?"

"It means that in all likelihood Lozupone thought the same thing we did, that is, that the protective railing was put up after the accident, but he let it slide."

"And why would he do that?"

"Maybe he was advised to stick to what Dipasquale and Spitaleri were telling him. But it's unlikely we'll ever find out who, in the commissariat or in the ministry of so-called justice, gave him this advice."

"Well, we might be able to get an idea, anyway," said Fazio.

"How?"

"Chief, you said you know Lozupone well. But do you know who he's married to?"

"No."

"Dr. Lattes's daughter."

"Ah."

Not bad, as news went.

Dr. Lattes, chief of the commissioner's cabinet, dubbed "Caffè-Lattes" for his cloying manner, was a man of church and prayer, a man who never said a word without first anointing it with lubricant, and who was continuously, at the right and wrong moments, giving thanks to the Blessed Virgin Mary.

"Do you know what political group Spitaleri's brother-in-law is with?"

"You mean the mayor? Mayor Alessandro is with the same party as the regional president, which happens to be the same party as Dr. Lattes, and he's the grand delegate of the Honorable M.P. Catapano, which is saying a lot."

Gerardo Catapano was a man who had managed to keep both the Cuffaros and the Sinagras, the two Mafia families of Vigàta, on good behavior.

Montalbano felt momentarily demoralized. How could it be that things never changed? Mutatis mutandis, one always ended up caught in dangerous webs of relations, collusions between the Mafia and politicians, the Mafia and entrepreneurs, politicians and banks, money-launderers and loan sharks.

What an obscene ballet! What a petrified forest of corruption, fraud, rackets, villainy, business! He imagined a likely dialogue:

"Proceed very carefully because Z, who is M.P. Y's man and the son-in-law of K, who is Mafia boss Z's man, enjoys particularly good relations with M.P. H.

"But doesn't M.P. H belong to the opposition party?"

"Yes, but it's the same thing."

How did Papa Dante put it?

> *Ah, servile Italy, you are sorrow's hostel,*
> *a ship without helmsman in terrible storms,*
> *lady not of the provinces, but of a brothel!*

Italy was still servile, obeying at least two masters, America and the Church, and the storms had become a daily occurrence thanks to a helmsman whom she would be better off without. Of course, the provinces of which Italy was the "lady" now numbered more than a hundred, but the brothel, for its part, had increased exponentially.

"So, about those six masons . . ." Fazio resumed.

"Wait. Have you got stuff to do this evening?"

"No, sir."

"Would you come with me to Montelusa?"

"What for?"

"To have a little chat with Filiberto, the watchman. I know how to find the worksite; Dipasquale explained it to me."

"It seems to me, sir, that you want to do harm to this Spitaleri."

"You've hit the nail on the head."

"Count me in."

"So, you going to tell me about these masons or not?"

Fazio gave him a dirty look.

"Chief, I've been trying to tell you for the past hour."

He unfolded his sheet of paper.

"The masons' names are as follows: Antonio Dalli Cardillo, Ermete Smecca, Ignazio Butera, Antonio Passalacqua, Stefano Fiorillo, Gaspare Miccichè. Dalli Cardillo and Miccichè are the two who worked up until the end and buried the illegal ground floor."

"If I ask you a question, will you answer me truthfully?"

"I'll try."

"Did you go dig up the complete vital statistics on each of these six masons?"

Fazio blushed slightly. He could not control his "records office mania," as the inspector called it.

"Yeah, Chief, I did. But I didn't read them to you."

"You didn't read them to me because you didn't have the courage. Did you find out if they're working now and where?"

"Of course. They're currently working at the four construction sites Spitaleri's got going."

"Four?"

"Yessir. And in five days another one's opening up. With the connections he's got between politicos and mafiosi, imagine the guy ever lacking work! Anyway, to conclude, Spitaleri told me he prefers always using the same masons."

"Except for the occasional Arab he can throw into the

garbage can without too much fuss. Are Dalli Cardillo and Miccichè working at the Montelusa site?"

"No."

"So much the better. I want you to call those two in for questioning tomorrow morning, one at ten and the other at noon, seeing that we'll probably be up late tonight. And don't accept any excuses. Threaten them if you need to."

"I'll get on it right away."

"Good. I'm going home. We'll meet back here at midnight, and then we'll head off to Montelusa."

"Okay. Should I put on my uniform?"

"You must be kidding. It's better if the guy thinks we're hoods."

Sitting on the veranda at Marinella, he thought he felt a hint of cool, but it was mostly a hypothesis of cool, since neither the sea nor the air was moving.

Adelina had made *pappanozza* for him. Onions and potatoes boiled a long time and mashed with the back of a fork until they blend together. Seasoning: olive oil, a hint of vinegar, salt, and freshly ground black pepper. It was all he ate. He wanted to keep to light food.

He sat outside until eleven o'clock, reading a good detective novel by two Swedish authors who were husband and wife, in which there wasn't a page without a ferocious and justified attack on social democracy and the government. In his mind Montalbano dedicated the book to all those who did not deign to read mystery novels because, in their opinion, they were only entertaining puzzles.

At eleven he turned on the television. *Lupus in fabula:* TeleVigàta featured a story showing the honorable Gerardo Catapano inaugurating the new municipal dog shelter of Montelusa.

He turned it off, freshened up a bit, and went out of the house.

He arrived at the station at a quarter to midnight. Fazio was already there. Each was wearing a light jacket over a short-sleeved shirt. They smiled at one another for having had the same idea. Anyone wearing a jacket in that extreme heat couldn't help but cause alarm, since ninety-nine times out of a hundred the jacket served to hide a revolver tucked into the waistband or pocket.

And, in fact, they were both armed.

"Shall we go in mine or yours?"

"Yours."

It took them scarcely half an hour to drive to the worksite, which was in the neighborhood of the old Montelusa train station.

They parked and got out. The worksite was surrounded by wooden fencing almost six and a half feet high and had a big, locked entrance gate.

"Do you remember," said Fazio, "what used to be here?"

"No."

"Palazzina Linares."

Montalbano remembered it. A little jewel from the second half of the nineteenth century which the Linares, rich sulfur merchants, had hired Giovan Battista Basile, the famous architect of the Teatro Massimo in Palermo, to build. Later the Linares had fallen into ruin, and so had their *palazzina*. Instead of restoring it, the authorities had decided to demolish it and build, in its place, an eight-story block of flats. So strict, that cultural ministry!

They walked up to the wooden gate, peered between the fenceposts, but saw no lights on.

Fazio pushed the gate softly three times.

"It's locked from the inside with a bolt."

"Think you could manage to climb over and open it?"

"Yeah, but not here. A car might drive by. I'll climb over the fencing in back and get in from there. You wait for me here."

"Be careful. There may be a dog."

"I don't think so. It would have already started barking."

The inspector had the time to smoke a cigarette before the gate opened just enough to let him in.

9

It was pitch-dark inside. To the right, however, one could make out a shed.

"I'll go get the flashlight," said Fazio.

When he returned, he relocked the gate with its bolt and turned on the flashlight. As they cautiously approached the door to the shed, they noticed that it was half open. Apparently, in this heat, Filiberto couldn't stand being inside with the door closed. Then they heard him snoring lustily.

"We mustn't give him any time to think," Montalbano whispered into Fazio's ear. "Don't turn on the lights. We'll work him over by the beam of the flashlight. We need to scare him to death."

"No problem," said Fazio.

They entered on tiptoe. Inside, the shed stank of sweat, and the smell of wine was so strong that one felt drunk just breathing it. Filiberto, in his underpants, was lying on a camping cot. He was the same man as in the dossier's photo.

Fazio shone the flashlight around the room. The watchman's clothes hung from a nail. There was a little table, two chairs, a small enamel washbasin on an iron tripod, and a jerry can. Montalbano grabbed it and smelled it: water. Without making any noise, he filled the basin, then picked it up in both hands, approached the cot and flung the water violently into Filiberto's face. The man opened his eyes and, blinded by Fazio's flashlight, shut them at once, then opened them again, raising a hand to shield himself.

"Who . . . who . . ."

"Whoopdeedoo!" said Montalbano. "Don't move."

And he brought his pistol into the beam of light. Filiberto instinctively put his hands up.

"You got a cell phone?" the inspector asked.

"Yes."

"Where is it?"

"In my jacket."

The one hanging from the nail. The inspector grabbed the cell phone, dropped it on the floor, and smashed it with his feet. Filiberto mustered the courage to ask:

"Who are you?"

"Friends, Filibè. Get up."

Filiberto stood up.

"Turn around."

His hands shaking slightly, Filiberto turned his back to them.

"But what do you want? Spitaleri's always paid his dues!"

"Shut up!" Montalbano ordered. "Say your prayers."

And he cocked the pistol.

Hearing that dry, metallic click, Filiberto's legs turned to pudding and he fell to his knees.

"For heaven's sake! I ain't done nothing! Why do you wanna kill me?" he asked, weeping.

Fazio gave him a kick in the shoulder, making him fall forward. Montalbano put the barrel of the pistol up against the nape of his neck.

"You listen to me . . ." he began.

Then he suddenly stopped.

"He's either dead or he just fainted."

He bent down to touch the jugular on the man's neck.

"He's fainted. Sit him up in a chair."

Fazio handed Montalbano the flashlight, grabbed the watchman by the armpits and sat him down. But he had to hold him up, because he kept sliding to one side. They both noticed that the man's underpants were wet. Filiberto had pissed himself in fear. Montalbano went up to him and dealt him such a slap that he reopened his eyes. The watchman blinked repeatedly, disoriented, then immediately started crying again.

"Don't kill me, please!"

"You answer our questions, you save your life," said Montalbano, holding the pistol to his face.

"I'll answer, I'll answer."

"When the Arab fell, was there any protective railing?"

"What Arab?"

Montalbano put the barrel to his forehead.

"When the Arab mason fell . . ."

"Ahh, yes—no, there wasn't."

"Did you put it up on Sunday morning?"

"Yessir."

"You, Spitaleri, and Dipasquale?"

"Yessir."

"Whose idea was it to douse the dead body with wine?"

"Spitaleri's."

"Now, be real careful and make no mistakes when you answer. Did you already have the materials for the railing here at the construction site?"

The question was essential to Montalbano. Everything hinged on the answer Filiberto would give.

"No, sir. Spitaleri ordered it, an' it was brought here early Sunday morning."

It was the best answer the inspector could ever want.

"Who supplied it? What company?"

"Ribaudo's."

"Did you sign the receipt?"

"Yessir."

Montalbano congratulated himself. He'd not only hit the nail right on the head, he had even found out what he wanted to know.

Now they needed to add some drama to the drama, for the benefit of the boss, Spitaleri.

"Why didn't you get the stuff from Milluso's?"

"How should I know?"

"And to think we told Spitaleri a thousand times, 'Ya gotta use Milluso's! Ya gotta use Milluso's! But, noooo ... He wants to play wise guy wit' us. He don't wanna understand. So now we's gonna kill you, just so he finally understands."

With the strength of desperation, Filiberto leapt to his feet. But he had no time to do anything else. Fazio, from behind, clubbed him on the side of the neck.

The watchman fell and didn't move.

They raced outside, opened the gate, got into the car, and as Fazio was turning on the ignition, Montalbano said:

"See how, if you're nice, you can have anything you want?"

Then he said no more.

As they were heading back to Vigàta, Fazio commented:

"That was just like an American movie!"

And, since the inspector just sat there in silence, he asked:

"Are you counting up how many crimes we committed?"

"It's better not to think about that."

"Are you dissatisfied with the answers Filiberto gave you?"

"No, on the contrary."

"So then, what's wrong?"

"I don't like what I did."

"I'm sure the guy didn't recognize us."

"Fazio, I didn't say we did something wrong, I said I didn't like it."

"You mean the way we treated Filiberto?"

"Yes."

"But, Chief, the guy's a criminal!"

"And we're not?"

"If we hadn't done what we did, he wouldn't have talked."

"That's not a good reason."

Fazio snapped.

"What do you want us to do, go back and tell him we're sorry?"

Montalbano said nothing.

A minute later, Fazio said:

"I apologize, sir."

"Oh, come on!"

"Do you think Spitaleri will swallow the story that we were sent by Milluso's outfit?"

"It'll take him two or three days to figure out that Milluso's had nothing to do with it. But those two or three days will be enough for me."

"There's one thing I still don't understand," said Fazio.

"Say it."

"Why, when he needed the material for the railing, did he turn to Ribaudo's instead of having it sent from one of his other worksites?"

"That would have meant involving other people from the other worksites. Spitaleri must have thought that the fewer the people who knew about the matter, the better. Apparently he could trust Ribaudo's."

During the night, Montalbano's conscience, contrary to his fears, chose to rest. Thus the inspector awoke from his five hours of sleep as if he had slept ten. The cloudless morning sky put him in a good mood. At that early hour, however, the air was already hot.

The minute he arrived at the office, he phoned Marshal

Alberto Laganà, of the Finance Police, who had helped him so many times before.

"Inspector! What a pleasant surprise! What's the good news?"

"It's bad news, unfortunately."

"Let's hear it anyway."

"Do you know the Ribaudo firm in Vigàta, the one that supplies construction materials?"

Laganà chuckled to himself.

"You bet we know them! Materials sold without invoices, evasion of sales tax, cooking the books . . . And we were just planning to renew the acquaintance in the next few days."

A stroke of excellent luck.

"When, exactly?"

"Three days from now."

"Couldn't you start early, say, tomorrow?"

"But tomorrow is August the fifteenth! What's this about?"

Montalbano explained the situation to him. And told him what he wanted to know.

"I think I can manage it the day after tomorrow," Laganà concluded.

"Chief? There's summon says he's called Falli Fardillo that says you summoned 'im for ten aclack this morning."

"Have you got the printout of the girl who was killed?"

"Yessir."

"Bring it to me, then tell Fazio to come to my office, and then, lastly, send that man in."

Naturally, Catarella sent in Dalli Cardillo first, then went and got the file, which Montalbano placed upside down on his desk, and finally went and called Fazio.

Dalli Cardillo was thickset and fiftyish, with short-cropped hair without a trace of white, swarthy, and sporting a moustache of the sort that Turks used to wear in the nineteenth century. He was nervous, and it showed.

But who isn't nervous when summoned without explanation to the police station? Wait a second. Without explanation? Was it possible Spitaleri hadn't already told him what to say?

"Mr. Dalli Cardillo, did Mr. Spitaleri tell you why you were summoned here?"

"Nossir."

He seemed sincere to Montalbano.

"Do you remember working on one of Spitaleri's sites six years ago, where you built a house in the Pizzo district of Marina di Montereale?"

Hearing the question, the mason looked so relieved that he allowed himself a little smile.

"So you discovered the illegal floor?" he asked.

"Yes."

"I did what the boss told me to do."

"I'm not accusing you of anything. All I want from you is some information."

"As far as that goes, I'm at your service."

"Was it you, together with your workmate, Gaspare Mic-cichè, who covered up the lower apartment with sandy soil?"

"Yessir."

"Did you work together the whole time?"

"No. On that day, I quit at twelve-thirty, and Miccichè continued alone."

"Why did you stop early?"

"Spitaleri's orders."

"But hadn't Spitaleri already left?"

"Yes, but the day before he left, he told us what to do."

"Could you explain to me how you went in and out of the bottom floor?"

"We made a sort of tunnel out of wooden planks, a kind of covered, sloping gangway, like for a steamship. Half of it was already covered up on top by all the soil. It led up to a window next to the smaller bathroom."

The window that Bruno had fallen into.

"How high was this tunnel?"

"It was low. Less than three feet. You had to stay down."

"Tell me something. What need was there for a tunnel?"

"Spitaleri told us to build one. He wanted the crew chief to check if the pressure of the soil could do any damage to the interior, letting the dampness inside and stuff like that."

"The crew chief was Dipasquale?"

"Yessir."

"And he came and checked?"

"Yessir. At the end of the first day. But he told us to keep working, because everything was okay."

"Did he also come by the last day?"

It was Fazio, cutting in.

"He didn't come by in the morning, when I was there. Maybe he did in the afternoon, but you'll have to ask Miccichè."

"You still haven't explained why you went home early."

"There wasn't much left to do. Just closing up a window with boards and plastic, taking apart the tunnel, and smoothing out the soil."

"Did you notice if there was a trunk in the living room?"

"Yessir. It was the owner that had us bring it down there, but I can't remember 'is name now. He had me and someone named Smecca carry it down."

"Was it empty?"

"Totally."

"Okay, thanks. You can go."

Dalli Cardillo couldn't believe it.

"A good day to you all!"

And he ran out.

"You know why Spitaleri didn't forewarn him of the interrogation and didn't tell him what to say?" asked Montalbano.

"No."

"Because the man is shrewd. He knows Dalli Cardillo is unaware of the murder. So he thought it was better if he showed up here with nothing to hide."

Gaspare Miccichè was a fortyish redhead who measured barely four feet eight inches tall. He had extremely long arms and bowed legs. He looked like a monkey. Surely Darwin, if he could have seen him, would have hugged him for joy. Miccichè must have been able to enter the wooden tunnel practically standing up. He, too, was a bit nervous.

"You're making me miss a whole morning of work!"

"Signor Miccichè, do you have any idea why we summoned you here?"

"I not only have an idea, I *know* why, because Spitaleri talked to me before I came. It's about that fucking illegal apartment."

"Didn't Spitaleri tell you anything else?"

"Why, what else is there?"

"Listen, on the twelfth of October, which was your last day of work, at what time did you go home?"

"It wasn't the last day. I went back the next day, too."

"To do what?"

"What I didn't do the afternoon of the day before."

"And what was that?"

"That afternoon, when I was getting back down to work, Dipasquale, the foreman, arrived and told me not to dismantle the tunnel."

"Why?"

"He said we'd better wait another day to see if there was any seepage. An' he also said the owner wanted to come by in the afternoon to check things himself."

"So what did you do?"

"What was I supposed to do? I left."

"Go on."

"That night, probably after nine o'clock, Dipasquale called me up saying I could take down the tunnel the following morning. So I went, I boarded up the window and covered it in plastic, then I dismantled the tunnel. I was just startin' to smooth out the ground when three guys from the team arrived."

"What team?"

"The ones that were supposed to remove the fencing from around the worksite. Then I went around the house twice with the grader and—"

"What's a grader?" asked Fazio.

"It's a machine like the one they use to make roads."

"A road-roller?"

"Yeah, but smaller. When I was done, I went back home."

"With the grader?"

"No, the guys from the team were supposed to take that away with their truck."

"Do you remember whether you entered the apartment for any reason on the morning of the thirteenth?"

"Spitaleri asked me the same question. Nah, I didn't go in 'cause there wasn't any reason to go in."

Had he gone in, he would have noticed at least the pool of blood in the living room. But he seemed sincere.

"Did you notice that there was a trunk in there?"

"Yessir. It was the owner—"

"Yes, Mr. Speciale had it brought down. Did you open it?"

"The trunk? No. I knew it was empty. Why would I open it?"

Without answering, Montalbano grabbed the printout, turned it over, and handed it to him.

Miccichè looked at the photograph of the murdered girl, noticed the date of her disappearance, and gave the printout back to the inspector. He looked genuinely stunned.

"What's that got to do with anything?"

It was Fazio who answered.

"If you had opened the trunk on the morning of the thirteenth, you would have found her inside it. Wrapped up in plastic, with her throat slashed."

Miccichè's reaction was not what they expected.

He shot straight to his feet, face turning purple, fists clenched, teeth bared. A wild animal. Montalbano was afraid he might jump onto the desk.

"Motherfucking son of a bitch!"

"Who?"

"Spitaleri! He knew and didn't tell me nothing! From the way he was talking to me, it's clear he wanted to get me in trouble!"

"Sit down and calm yourself. Why, in your opinion, would Spitaleri have wanted to get you in trouble?"

"To make you guys think it was me who killed that girl! When I went home that day, I left Dipasquale there! I don't know nothing at all about any of this!"

"Did you ever see this girl anywhere around the construction site?"

"Never!"

"When you stopped working on the afternoon of the twelfth, do you remember what you did?"

"How could I possibly remember? You're talking about six years ago!"

"Make an effort, Signor Miccichè. It's in your own interest," said Fazio.

Miccichè was seized by another fit of rage. He leapt to his feet and, before Fazio could stop him, he set off at a run and butted his head mightily against the closed door of the office. As Fazio was sitting him back down by force, the door opened and there appeared a befuddled Catarella.

"D'jou call for me, Chief?"

10

Between words and shoves, blandishments and brandishings of handcuffs, Fazio and Montalbano finally managed to get the unchained beast to calm down. Then, after some five minutes of good behavior, head in his hands, concentrating as he tried to remember, Miccichè began to mutter.

"Wait a minute . . . wait a minute . . ."

"The head-butt is bringing his memory back," the inspector said to Fazio under his breath.

"Wait a minute . . . I think it was the same day that . . . Yes . . . Yes . . ."

He leapt to his feet yet again, but Montalbano and Fazio were quick to jump on him and immobilize him. By now they'd learned the technique.

"But I just wanted to call my wife!"

"Well, if that's all . . ." said the inspector.

Fazio held out the phone with the outside line for him. Miccichè dialed a number but was too nervous and got it wrong, reaching a grocer's shop. He dialed again and got it wrong again.

"Let me dial it for you."

Miccichè told him the number, holding the receiver in his hand.

"Carmelina? 'Ss me. D'you remember six years ago, when our boy Michilino broke 'is leg? Never mind why I'm asking you. Just say yes or no. Do you remember? You don't remember if it was six years ago? Think hard. Yes? And didn't it happen on the twelfth of October? Yes?"

He hung up.

"Now iss all comin' back to me. Since I got home early that day, I laid down and went to sleep. Then Carmelina woke me up, crying. Michilino had fallen off 'is bike and broke 'is leg. So I took 'im to Montelusa hospital an' my wife came wit' me. We stayed at the hospital until that evening. You can check."

"That's what we're gonna do," said Fazio.

He exchanged a glance with Montalbano.

"For now, you can go," said the inspector.

"Thanks. I'm gonna go bust Spitaleri's face, even if it costs me my job!"

And he left the room grinding his teeth.

"He acts like he escaped from some cage at the zoo," commented Fazio.

"Why do you think Spitaleri didn't tell him anything about the murder?" the inspector asked him.

"Because Spitaleri, having already left, had no way of knowing that Miccichè's kid broke his leg. He was convinced he didn't have an alibi."

"So, in short, Miccichè was right: Spitaleri wanted to set him up. But the question is: why?"

"Maybe because he thinks Dipasquale is involved. And Spitaleri cares more about Dipasquale, who probably knows a thing or two about him, than about some poor bastard like Miccichè."

"Right."

"What should I do? Call Dipasquale back in?"

"You got some doubts about him?"

Thus the foreman also entered the game.

───

Before going out to eat at the usual place, Enzo's trattoria, the inspector stopped in front of Catarella's closet, and the switchboard operator sprang to attention.

"At ease. What ever happened with those fans?"

"Can't be found anywheres, Chief. Not even in Montelusa. They says they should have 'em in tree or four days' time."

"Time enough for us to be properly roasted."

Catarella accompanied him to the door and stood there watching him.

The blast of heat that came out of his car when Montalbano opened the door discouraged him from entering. Maybe it was better just to walk to Enzo's, which was about fifteen minutes away on foot, taking, naturally, the sides of the streets that were in shade. He headed off.

"Chief! What, you goin' on foot?"

"Yes."

"Wait a second."

Catarella went back into the station and came out with a small green cap with a visor, like baseball players wear. He handed it to the inspector.

"Here, put this on to cover your head."

"Oh, come on!"

"Chief! You're gonna get sunstricken!"

"Better sunstroke than looking like somebody going to the Pontida meetings."

"Where you going, Chief?"

"Never mind."

After he'd been walking five minutes with his head down, he heard a voice:

"*Vocumprà?*"

He looked up. An Arab selling sunglasses, straw hats, bathing suits. Next to his face, however, the man was holding a gadget that caught the inspector's attention, a sort of portable minifan that must have functioned with batteries.

"I'll take that," he said, pointing to the fan.

"This is mine for me."

"Haven't you got another one?"

"No."

"Come on, how much you want for it?"

"Fifty euros."

Fifty euros was way too much.

"Let's make it thirty."

"Forty."

Montalbano paid him the forty euros, grabbed the little fan, and resumed walking, holding the gadget next to his face. He couldn't believe it—it actually cooled him off very nicely.

Sitting down to eat, however, he wanted to keep to light things and had only a main course. And, thanks to the little fan, he was able to take his customary walk along the jetty and sit for a short while on the flat rock.

The minifan came equipped with a clamp, which allowed the inspector to attach it to the edge of the desk. There was no doubt about it: The thing did provide a bit of relief to the overheated office.

"Catarella!"

"Behole the brillince o' man!" Catarella commented in admiration upon seeing the little fan.

"Fazio here?"

"Yessir."

"Tell him to come in."

Fazio also congratulated him on the contraption.

"How much did you pay for it?"

"Ten euros."

He was embarrassed to admit he'd paid forty.

"Where'd you buy it? I want to get one myself."

"Some Arab passing through. Unfortunately it was the only one he had."

The telephone rang.

It was Dr. Pasquano. The inspector turned on the speakerphone so Fazio could also hear.

"You all right, Montalbano?"

"Yes, why do you ask?"

"Well, considering the fact that you didn't bust my balls this morning, I was worried."

"Did you perform the autopsy?"

"Why else would I be calling you? To hear your lovable, mellifluous voice?"

He must have discovered something important to have called him at all.

"Tell me about it."

"Well, first of all, the girl had completely digested what she had eaten, but had not yet evacuated. Therefore she was killed either around six o'clock in the evening, or later, around eleven."

"I think it was around six in the evening."

"That's your business."

"Is there anything else?"

The doctor didn't like saying what he was about to say.

"I was wrong."

"About what?"

"The girl was a virgin. Beyond a shadow of a doubt."

Montalbano and Fazio looked at each other in astonishment.

"What does that mean?" asked the inspector.

"You don't know what being a virgin means? Well, you must know that women who haven't yet—"

"You know perfectly well what I was referring to, Doctor." Montalbano didn't feel like kidding around. Pasquano said nothing. "If the girl died a virgin, it means the motive for the murder is not what we thought."

"Did you know you're an Olympic champion?"

Montalbano looked dumbfounded.

"Explain yourself."

"You're a champion in the hundred-meter dash."

"Why?"

"You're running too hard, my friend. Going too fast. It's not your job to reach an immediate conclusion. What's happening to you?"

What's happening to me is that I've grown old, thought the inspector, *and I want to reach a quick conclusion on a case that's been weighing on me.*

"So," Pasquano resumed, "I can confirm that, at the moment she was killed, the girl was in the position I said she was in."

"Then explain to me why the murderer had her assume that position, after having forced her to strip, if he wasn't going to screw her?"

"Since we didn't find any clothes, we can't know whether the killer forced her to strip before he killed her or stripped her himself afterward. Anyway, the question of her clothes is unimportant, Montalbano."

"You think so?"

"Of course! As unimportant as the fact that he wrapped up the body and put it in the trunk!"

"He didn't do it to hide her?"

"Do you know, Montalbano, you don't seem to be in very good form?"

"Maybe it's my age, Doctor."

"What! The killer's going to take the trouble to put the body into a trunk while leaving a puddle of blood as big as a lake a couple of yards away?"

"Well, then, why, in your opinion, did he put her in the trunk?"

"With all the murders you've handled, you're asking me? To hide her from himself, my dear inspector, not from us! It's a sort of concrete, immediate repression of reality!"

Pasquano was right.

How often had they come across amateur murderers who covered the victim's face, especially if it was a woman, with the first thing at hand—a rag, a towel, a sheet?

"You have to start with the only sure thing we've got," the doctor continued, "which is the girl's position when the killer cut her throat. If you concentrate a little, you'll see that—"

"I understand what you're trying to say."

"If you finally understand, then tell me."

"That maybe the killer, at the final moment, was no longer able to rape her, and so, in the throes of an uncontrollable rage, he pulled out the knife . . ."

"Which, as they tell us in psychoanalysis, is a substitute for the penis. Very good."

"Did I pass the exam?"

"Well, there may be another hypothesis," Pasquano continued.

"What would that be?"

"That the killer sodomized her."

"My God," Fazio muttered.

"What?" The inspector rebelled. "You fill my ears with idle chatter for half an hour and only deign to tell me at the end what you should have told me from the start?"

"It's just that I wasn't one hundred percent sure. I wasn't able to establish the fact with any real certainty. Too much time has passed. But, based on certain, very small signs, I would lean towards the affirmative. Mind you, I said I *would* lean. Conditional tense."

"So, in short, you don't feel you could go from the conditional to another verb tense, such as the present indicative."

"Frankly, no."

"It keeps getting worse and worse," Fazio said bitterly, when the inspector hung up.

Montalbano remained pensive.

Fazio continued.

"Chief, do you remember when you said to me that when you catch the killer, you want to smash his face in?"

"Yes. And I reiterate the promise."

"Can I join the party?"

"You're perfectly welcome to. Did you summon Dipasquale?"

"For six o'clock this evening, after he gets off work."

As Fazio was leaving the room, the telephone rang again.

"Chief? Iss Proxecutor Dommaseo onna line."

"Put him on," said Montalbano. Then, to Fazio: "You listen, too," and he turned the speakerphone back on.

"Montalbano?"

"Judge?"

"I wanted to let you know that I've been to the Morreale home to give them the terrible news."

His voice was sorrowful, emotional.

"That was very good of you, sir."

"It was awful, you know."

"I can imagine."

Tommaseo, however, wanted to tell him about his ordeal.

"Poor Signora Francesca, the mother, fainted. And the father, you wouldn't believe it, he started wandering about the house, talking to himself, and couldn't stand on his own two feet."

Tommaseo was waiting for a comment from Montalbano, who obliged him.

"Poor things!"

"They'd been hoping, for all these years, that their daughter was still alive . . . What's the expression? That hope—"

"—is always the last thing to die," Montalbano finished his sentence, obliging him again and cursing himself for using a cliché.

"That's so true, dear Montalbano."

"So they were in no condition to identify the body."

"No, it was identified, anyway! The dead girl is indeed Caterina Morreale!"

Montalbano and Fazio looked at each other in bewilderment. Why was Tommaseo suddenly twittering like a bird? It wasn't such a pleasant matter he had dealt with, after all.

"I made a point of taking Adriana myself in my car," Tommaseo continued.

"Wait a second. Who's Adriana?"

"What do you mean, who's Adriana? Wasn't it you who told me the victim had a twin sister?"

Montalbano and Fazio looked at each other in disbelief. What was the guy talking about? Maybe he was trying to turn the inspector's trick against him?

"You were right," Tommaseo continued, his tone now one of excitement, as if he'd just won the lottery. "The girl is absolutely gorgeous!"

That certainly explained the twittering!

"She studies medicine at Palermo, did you know? Mostly, she's a really strong girl with a lot of character, even though, after identifying the body, she had a little crisis and I had to comfort her."

One can only imagine just how ready the good prosecutor was to comfort her, and with every means at his disposal.

They said good-bye and hung up.

"But that's not possible!" said Fazio. "You must have known there was a twin sister!"

"I swear to you I didn't. But it's an important thing to know. The victim probably confided in her. Could you call up the Morreale home and ask if I can drop in tomorrow morning around ten?"

"Even though it's August fifteenth?"

"Where do you think they're gonna go? They're in mourning."

Fazio went out and came back five minutes later.

"You know what? Adriana herself answered the phone! She said it's probably better if you don't go to their place. Her parents are feeling very bad and they're not in any condition to talk. She suggested she come here herself, to the station, at the same time tomorrow morning."

As the inspector was waiting for Dipasquale, he phoned the Aurora Real Estate agency.

"Signor Callara? Montalbano here."

"Is there any news, Inspector?"

"I haven't got any. How about you?"

"Yes, I do."

"I bet you informed Signora Gudrun Speciale about the illegal floor we discovered."

"Good guess! I called her the moment I recovered a little from the shock I got opening that trunk. Damn my curiosity!"

"What can you do, Signor Callara? That's just the way it goes, unfortunately."

"I've always been curious! You know, one time, when I was still a kid—"

"But you were telling me about your phone call to Signora Gudrun ..."

The last thing he needed was to hear about Signor Callara's childhood memories.

"Ah, yes. But I didn't tell her about the poor girl who was killed."

"You were right. What did Signora Gudrun decide?"

"She instructed me to take the necessary steps to obtain amnesty, and to send her the papers so she can sign them."

"That sounds like the most sensible thing."

"Yes, except that in the fax she sent me, she also wrote that, afterwards, she's going to give me authorization to sell. But you know what I say? I've got half a mind to buy that house myself. What do you think?"

"You're the real estate agent, I'm sure you'll make the right decision. Good day."

"Wait. There's another thing I have to tell you. Since I was honestly advising her not to sell the house ..."—honestly in the sense that, if she sold it, Callara would lose his percentage of the rent—"... she replied that she didn't want to hear about it anymore."

"Did you ask her why?"

"Yes. She said she would write to me about it. And, just this morning, a fax came in explaining why she wants to sell. I think this fax might be of interest to you."

"To me?"

"Yes. She says her son, Ralf, is dead."

"What?!"

"Yes, they found his remains about two months ago."

"His remains? What, you mean he died a long time ago?"

"Yes. Apparently Ralf died on his way back to Cologne with Mr. Speciale. She even sent a German newspaper clipping with a translation."

"When can I see it?"

"This evening, when I close up the office. I'll come by the station and drop it off with the guy at the entrance."

And why had it taken them six years to find this other body, or what remained of it?

11

The look Dipasquale gave him upon entering the inspector's office was more surly than ever.

"Please sit down."

"Will this take long?"

"As long as is needed. Mr. Dipasquale, before we talk about the house in Pizzo, I'd like to ask you, now that I've got you here, where and how I might find the watchman of the construction site in Montelusa."

"Are you still stuck on that damned business about the Arab? Inspector Lozupone himself—"

Montalbano pretended he hadn't heard his colleague's name mentioned.

"Tell me where I can find him. And give me his name and surname again. You told me last time, but I forgot them since I didn't write them down. Fazio, be sure to make a note of this."

"Right away, Inspector."

Not bad, as improvised theater.

"Inspector, I'll tell the watchman myself that you want to talk to him. His name's Filiberto Attanasio."

"I'm sorry, but how are you going to contact him when the worksite is closed?"

"He's got a cell phone."

"Please give me the number."

"It doesn't work. The other night ... the other day, I mean, it fell on the ground and broke."

"Okay, then tell him directly yourself."

"All right, but I should warn you, he won't be able to come for two or three days."

"Why not?"

"He's had an attack of malaria."

They must have scared the watchman pretty good.

"Tell you what. When he's feeling better, ask him to give us a call. Now, back to us. I had you come in because this morning I questioned two masons, named Dalli Cardillo and Miccichè, who worked on the house in Pizzo—"

"Inspector, don't waste your breath. I know exactly what happened."

"Who told you?"

"Spitaleri. Miccichè burst into his office acting like he was out of his mind and punched him so hard he gave him a bloody nose. He was convinced Spitaleri wanted to frame him. The guy oughta be caged up with wild animals! Well, now he can start panhandling, 'cause it ain't gonna be easy for him to find any more work as a mason."

"Spitaleri's not the only builder in town," said Fazio.

"Yeah, but all it takes is a word from me or Spitaleri—"

"—to put him out on the streets?"

"You said it."

"I shall make a note of what you just said and take proper action," said Montalbano.

"What's that mean?" asked Dipasquale, alarmed.

More than the threatening tone, what most frightened him was the inspector's formality.

"It means that you said, in our presence, that you will see to it that Miccichè remains unemployed. You threatened a witness."

"Witness? What witness? I think you mean witless!"

"I won't have you speaking that way to me!"

"And anyway, if I'm threatening him, iss not for what he said here, but for punching Spitaleri!"

Quick and clever, was the foreman.

"For now, let's not get off the subject. Spitaleri told us that work on the Pizzo house ended on the twelfth of October. Which you confirmed. Whereas the work didn't end until the morning of the following day, as we found out from Miccichè."

"What's the difference?"

"That's up to us to decide. Spitaleri could not have known that the work carried over into the next day, because he'd already left. But did you know?"

"Yes."

"In fact, wasn't it you yourself who made the decision to prolong it?"

"Yes."

"Why didn't you tell us?"

"It slipped my mind."

"Are you sure?"

"Anyway, last time I came in, you didn't tell me about the girl that was killed."

He was trying to counterattack, the asshole.

"Dipasquale, we're not here to play 'you tell me one thing, and I'll tell you another.' At any rate, when you walked in, you already knew, of course, about the dead girl, because Spitaleri had told you about her. And yet you acted as if nothing had happened."

"What was I supposed to say? Nothing?"

"Not at all! You did say something."

"What?"

"You tried to create an alibi for yourself. You said that four days before the work in Pizzo was completed, Spitaleri sent you to Fela to start on a new worksite. So, why is it that, on the eleventh and twelfth of October, in the afternoon, you were at Pizzo and not in Fela?"

Dipasquale didn't even try to come up with an excuse.

"Inspector, you gotta understand. I got really scared when Spitaleri told me about the dead body. So I made up that story about being sent to Fela. But I figured that sooner or later you's gonna find out it was a lie."

"Then tell us exactly what happened."

"Well, at eleven o'clock I went into that goddamned apartment. I wanted to see if it was damp or if there was any seepage. I even went into the living room, but I didn't see nothing strange."

"What about the next day, the twelfth?"

"I went back there in the afternoon. I told Miccichè not

to dismantle the tunnel. Then he left and I stayed another half hour to wait for Mr. Speciale."

"Did you go inside to check on everything?"

"Yessir. An' everything was in order."

"In the living room, too?" asked Fazio.

"In the living room, too."

"And then?"

"Finally, Mr. Speciale arrived."

"How did he come?"

"By car. He'd rented it when he got here."

"Was his stepson with him?"

"Yessir."

"What time was it?"

"Probably 'round four."

"Did you go downstairs?"

"All three of us."

"How were you able to see?"

"I had a powerful flashlight. And Speciale had one, too. Speciale checked everything very closely. He's a real fussy man. A stickler. Then I asked him if we could close up the passage and level the ground, and he said okay. He gave one last look, and then we went outside, Mr. Speciale and me. We said good-bye, and I left."

"What about Ralf?"

"The kid asked his stepfather for the flashlight and stayed downstairs."

"To do what?"

"Dunno. He just liked being underground. He looked at

all the wrapped-up casings and laughed. Didn't I tell you he was crazy?"

"So, when you left, Speciale and Ralf stayed behind in Pizzo?"

"That's where I left 'em. Anyways, Speciale had the keys to the apartment, which was habitable."

"Do you remember more or less what time it was when you left?"

"Around five o'clock."

"Why did you wait until nine o'clock that night to inform Miccichè that he could take down the tunnel?"

"I called him at least three times, and there was never any answer! I didn't reach him till evening!"

It made sense. Miccichè and his wife had spent the afternoon and early evening at Montelusa Hospital.

"What did you do after you left Pizzo?"

Dipasquale gave a slight chuckle.

"You want an alibi?"

"You're better off if you've got one."

"I got one. I went into Spitaleri's office. He was supposed to be calling us—the secretary and me—between six and eight o'clock."

"But he hadn't landed in Bangkok yet!" said Fazio.

"Of course not. But the flight was making a stop in some place whose name I can't remember. Spitaleri knows the route. He goes to those places often."

"Did he call?"

"Yes."

"Was it an important phone call?"

"It was pretty important. It was about a government contract we was supposed to be getting. If we got it, then I would have to take care of a few things."

Such as, for example, doling out to the Sinagras, the Cuffaros, the mayor, and anyone else in charge the wads of bills they had coming to them, thought the inspector. But he didn't say anything.

"So, I'm curious to know, did you get it?" asked Fazio.

"By the twelfth they hadn't decided yet. They decided on the fourteenth."

"In your favor?" Fazio asked again.

"Yes."

How could you go wrong?

"And did you tell Spitaleri?"

"Yes, the following day. We called him ourselves at his hotel in Bangkok."

"Who's 'we'?"

"The secretary and me. Anyways, to conclude, if you wanna know what happened at Pizzo after I left, you'll have to call Mr. Speciale in Germany."

"Don't you know? He's dead."

"What? D'he have a heart attack?"

"No, he fell down the stairs at his home."

"Well, you can always ask Ralf."

"Ralf's dead, too. I just found out half an hour ago."

Dipasquale balked.

"Wha . . . aat?"

"He got on the train with his stepfather but never got to Cologne. He must have fallen off."

"So that house in Pizzo is cursed!" the foreman said, disturbed.

You're telling me! Montalbano thought to himself.

The inspector grabbed the printout with the photo on his desk and handed it to him. Dipasquale took it, looked at the photograph, and his face turned flaming red.

"Do you know her?"

"Yes. She's one of the twin girls who lived in the last house on the dirt road at Pizzo, before the one we built."

So that was why the missing-persons report was made in Fiacca. At the time, Montereale fell within its jurisdiction.

"This is the girl that was killed?" asked Dipasquale, still holding the printout in his hand.

"Yes."

"I am positive that . . ."

"Speak."

"You remember what I told you last time? This is the girl Ralf chased around naked and that Spitaleri saved."

Suddenly Dipasquale realized he'd made a mistake. Talking without thinking, he'd dragged Spitaleri into it. He tried to set things right.

"Or maybe not. In fact, there's no 'maybe' about it. I got it wrong. This is the twin sister, I'm sure of it."

"Did you see the twins often?"

"Often, no. Now and then. There was no way to get to Pizzo without driving by their house."

"How come Miccichè said he'd never seen her before?"

"Inspector, the masons would come to the worksite at seven o'clock in the morning, when I'm sure the girls were still asleep. An' they got off work at five-thirty, when the girls were still down on the beach. But me, I would go back and forth, to and from the worksite."

"How about Spitaleri?"

"He came less often."

"Thanks, you can go," Montalbano concluded.

"What do you make of Dipasquale's alibi?" Fazio asked after the foreman had left.

"It could be true or it could be false. It rests entirely on a phone call from Spitaleri that we don't know was ever really made."

"We could ask the secretary."

"Are you kidding? The secretary will do and say exactly what Spitaleri tells her to do and say. Otherwise she'll find herself one hundred percent sacked. And with the shortage of work these days, don't imagine she's gonna put her job in jeopardy."

"I get the feeling we're not making any progress."

"I've got the same feeling. Tomorrow we'll hear what Adriana has to say."

"Would you explain to me why you want to talk to Filiberto?"

"But I don't want to talk to him. I just wanted to see what Dipasquale's reaction would be. Whether he had any suspicions about us being the two who paid Filiberto a visit the other night."

"It looks to me like we haven't entered their minds."

"Sooner or later they'll come to that conclusion."

"And what will they do then?"

"In my opinion, they won't show their hand. Spitaleri will go complain to his little friends who protect him, and they'll do something."

"Like what?"

"Fazio, we'll wait for them to come and bust our heads, and then we'll start crying."

"Okay," Fazio began, "I'm gonna g——"

A boom as loud as a cannon blast interrupted him. It was the door slamming against the wall. Catarella was standing there with one arm raised and his fist closed, holding an envelope in his other hand.

"Sorry 'bout the noise, Chief. Somebuddy just now brought a litter."

"Give it to me and get out of here before I shoot you."

It was a big envelope, and in it were two pages faxed from Germany and addressed to Callara's agency.

"Stay and listen, Fazio. This contains the news of Ralf's death. Callara sent it over to me."

Montalbano began reading aloud.

Dear Sir,

Three months ago, while reading a newspaper, I happened to notice a news item, of which I am herewith sending you a copy with accompanying translation.

I immediately felt, perhaps by maternal instinct, that those wretched remains must belong to my poor Ralf, for whom I have been waiting all these long years.

I asked that a comparison be made between the unknown

man's DNA and my son's. It was not at all easy to obtain consent for such a test; I had to insist for a long time.

Finally, a few days ago, the result was sent to me.

The data correspond perfectly. Beyond a shadow of a doubt, those remains belong to my late son, Ralf.

Since no trace of clothing was found, the police maintain that Ralf got up in the night to go to the bathroom during his train journey home from Italy, accidentally opened the outside door, and fell out.

That house in Sicily has brought us nothing but misfortune. It led to the death of both my son, Ralf, and my husband, Angelo, who after his trip to Sicily, and certainly after Ralf's disappearance, was no longer the same man.

For this reason, I would like to sell the house.

Sometime in the next few days I will fax you copies of all the documents related to the house's construction: the blueprints, the permit, the Land Registry plan, and the contracts with Spitaleri Enterprises. You will need these for the amnesty request as well as for the future sale.

Gudrun Walser

The translation of the news item went as follows:

REMAINS OF UNIDENTIFIED MAN FOUND

The day before yesterday, following a fire that broke out in the dense brush on a railway embankment some twenty kilometers outside of Köln, the remains of a human body were discovered in a half-buried recess in the ground by

firemen who had rushed to the scene to control the flames.
The man's identity could not be established, however, as no
clothing or documents were found in the vicinity.

The autopsy revealed beyond a doubt that the remains
belonged to a young man, and that the death dated from at
least five years ago.

"This fall from the train doesn't convince me," said
Fazio.

"Me neither. The police say Ralf got up to go to the
john. What, is he gonna do it naked? What if he runs into
someone in the corridor?"

"So what do you think?"

"Bah. It's all guesswork, as you know. We'll never have
any proof or confirmation. Maybe Ralf spotted a pretty girl
on the train and decided to strip down naked and try to kiss
her, the way Dipasquale said he used to do. And maybe he
ran into her husband, father, or boyfriend, who threw his ass
out of the train window."

"That sounds like a bit of a stretch to me."

"There's another possible explanation. Suicide."

"For what reason?"

"Let's make an argument based on the fact that, on the
afternoon of October the twelfth, Angelo Speciale and his
stepson remained in Pizzo alone, as Dipasquale says. Say Angelo goes out onto the terrace to enjoy the sunset, while Ralf
goes for a walk in the direction of the Morreale house. Don't
forget that Dipasquale told us that Ralf had tried to grab Rina
once. He happens to run into her, and this time he doesn't

want to let her get away. He threatens the girl with a knife and forces her to go with him into the underground apartment. And that's where the tragedy occurs. Ralf wraps up the girl's body, puts it in the trunk, takes her clothes, hides them in the house, and then goes out on the terrace to keep Angelo company. The stepfather, however, finds the girl's clothes, maybe on their last day there. Maybe they were even stained with her blood when he was killing her."

"But hadn't he made her take her clothes off?"

"We don't know. It's possible he only stripped her afterwards. There was no need for her to be completely naked for him to do what he wanted to do."

"So how does it end?"

"It ends as follows: During the train ride back to Germany, Angelo forces Ralf to confess to the murder. And, after confessing, the kid kills himself by jumping off the train. But I can give you a variant, if you like."

"What?"

"Angelo himself throws him off the train, killing the monster."

"Pretty far-fetched, Chief!"

"Whatever the case, don't forget that Signora Gudrun wrote that when her husband got back to Cologne, he said he never wanted to leave again. Something must therefore have happened to him."

"You're damn right something happened to him. The poor guy woke up the next morning in his sleeper car and his stepson was gone!"

"In short, you don't see Speciale as a murderer?"

"No way."

"But, you know, in Greek tragedy—"

"We're in Vigàta, Chief, not Greece."

"Tell me the truth: Do you like the story or don't you?"

"It seems okay for TV."

12

It had been a long day, made longer by the August heat. The inspector felt a little tired. But he had no lack of appetite.

When he opened the oven, he was disappointed not to find anything. But when he opened the refrigerator, he saw a sort of salad of calamari, celery, and tomatoes that still needed to be dressed with olive oil and lemon. Adelina had wisely prepared him a dish to be eaten cold.

A mild, newborn breeze was circulating out on the veranda. It was too feeble to move the dense mass of heat that was still holding out as night fell, but it was better than nothing.

He took off his clothes, put on a bathing suit, ran down to the water, and dived in. He went for a long swim, taking broad, slow strokes. Returning to shore, he went into the house, set the little table on the veranda, and began to eat. When he had finished, he still felt hungry, so he prepared a plate of green olives, cured black *passuluna* olives, and caciocavallo cheese that called for—indeed demanded—good wine.

The light breeze on the veranda had matured from infancy to adolescence and was making itself felt.

He decided to seize a favorable moment when his thoughts weren't logjammed from the heat, and tried to think rationally about the investigation he had on his hands. He cleared the little table of dishes, cutlery, and glasses, and replaced these with a few sheets of paper.

Since he didn't like to take notes, he decided to write himself a letter, as he sometimes did.

Dear Montalbano,

I find myself forced to point out that, either from the onset of a senile second childhood or because of the intense heat of the last few days, your thoughts have lost all their luster and become extremely opaque and slow-moving. You had a chance to see this for yourself during your dialogue with Dr. Pasquano, who easily got the better of you in that exchange.

Pasquano presented two hypotheses concerning the fact that the killer took away the girl's clothes: one, it was an irrational act; and two, the killer took them because he's a fetishist. Both hypotheses are plausible.

But there is a third possibility. It occurred to you as you were talking to Fazio, and that is that the killer took the clothes because they were stained with blood. Stained with the blood that had spouted from the girl's throat as he was killing her.

But things may well have gone differently. You need to take a step back.

Neither when you discovered the body yourself, nor when you had Callara discover it officially, did you see the giant bloodstain near the French door, and you didn't see it for the simple reason that it wasn't visible to the naked eye. The Forensics team only noticed it because they used luminol.

If the killer had left the big stain exactly the way it had formed on the floor, some traces of dried blood would have remained on the tiles, even six years later. Whereas, in fact, nothing was found.

What does this mean?

It means that the man, after killing the girl, wrapping her up, and sticking her in the trunk, used her clothes to wipe up, however superficially, the pool of blood. He dampened her clothes with a little water, since the faucets were in working order, then he put them in a plastic bag that he'd found there or brought along with him.

Now the question is: Why didn't he get rid of the clothes by simply throwing the bag on top of the corpse?

And the answer is: Because in order to do this, he would have had to reopen the trunk.

And this was impossible for him, because it would have meant having a reality he had already begun to repress thrown back in his face. Pasquano is right: He hid the body not to keep us from seeing it, but to keep himself from seeing it.

There's still another important question. It's already been asked, but it's worth repeating: Was it necessary to kill the girl? And, if so, why?

As for the "why," Pasquano hinted at the possibility of blackmail, or a fit of temporary insanity from the rage at finding himself suddenly impotent.

My answer is: Yes, it was necessary. But for only one, completely different, reason.

The following: The girl knew her aggressor well.

The killer must have forced the girl to enter the underground apartment with him, and once she was down there, her fate was sealed. For if the man had left her alive, she would surely have accused him of rape or attempted rape. Thus, when the killer brought her underground, he already knew that, in addition to raping her, he would also have to murder her. On this point, there could be no more doubt. Premeditated murder.

Then comes the mother of all questions: Who is the killer? One must proceed by elimination.

It definitely could not be Spitaleri. Even though you can't stand the guy, and even though you'll try to screw him on some other charge, there is one incontrovertible fact: On the afternoon of the twelfth, Spitaleri was not in Pizzo, but on a flight for Bangkok. And bear in mind that for Spitaleri, a girl Rina's age was already too mature for his tastes.

Miccichè has an alibi: He spent the afternoon at Montelusa Hospital. You can have this verified, if you like, but it would be a waste of time.

Dipasquale says he has an alibi. He left Pizzo around five in the afternoon and went to Spitaleri's office to receive his boss's phone call. At nine P.M., he spoke with Miccichè. But he didn't tell us what he did after going to Spitaleri's office. He said he and his boss had agreed he would call between six and eight o'clock. Let's say for the sake of argument that the phone call comes in at six-thirty. Dipasquale leaves the office and happens to run into Rina. He knows her, asks her if she wants a ride back to Pizzo. The girl accepts and . . . That leaves Dipasquale plenty of time to call Miccichè by nine.

Ralf. He stayed behind in Pizzo with his stepfather after Dipasquale left. He knows Rina, has already tried to assault her. What if things actually did happen the way you told Fazio? The mystery of his death remains, and could be linked in some way to his guilt. But accusing Ralf would be, for all intents and purposes, an act of faith. He's dead, his stepfather is dead. Neither of the two could tell us what happened.

In conclusion: Dipasquale should be the number-one suspect. But you're not convinced.

A big hug and take care.

> *Yours,*
> *Salvo*

He was taking off his bathing suit, getting ready to go to bed when, all of a sudden, he felt like talking to Livia. He dialed the number of her cell phone. It rang a long time, but nobody picked up.

How was that possible? Was Massimiliano's boat so big that Livia couldn't hear her cell phone ring? Or was she too engaged, too busy doing other things to answer the phone?

He was about to hang up in anger when he heard Livia's voice.

"Hello? Who is it?"

What did she mean, "Who is it?" Couldn't she read the caller's number on the display or whatever the hell it was called?

"It's Salvo."

"Oh, it's you."

Not disappointed. Indifferent.

"What were you doing?"

"Sleeping."

"Where?"

"On the deck. I fell asleep without realizing it. It's all so peaceful, so beautiful . . ."

"Where are you?"

"We're sailing towards Sardinia."

"And where's Massimiliano?"

"He was right beside me when I fell asleep. Now I think he's—"

He cut off the call, pulling out the plug.

And what was that fucking asshole Massimiliano doing there? Singing her a lullaby?

He went to bed with his hair standing on end.

And it took the hand of God for him to fall asleep.

━━━

In vain he went for another swim after waking; in vain he got into the shower, which should have been cold but was actually hot because the water in the tanks on the roof was so torrid you could have boiled pasta in it; in vain he dressed as lightly as possible.

The moment he set foot outside the house, he had to admit to himself that it was no use. The heat was a fiery blaze.

He went back into the house, stuck a shirt, underpants, and pair of trousers as thin as onionskin in a shopping bag, and left.

He arrived at the station with his shirt drenched in sweat and his underpants all of a piece with the skin of his ass, so tightly were they sticking.

Cataralla tried to stand up and salute, but couldn't manage, falling lifelessly back into his chair.

"Ah, Chief, Chief! I'm dying! 'Ss the devil, this heat!"

"Suck it up!"

He went and slipped into the bathroom. He took all his clothes off, washed himself, pulled out the shirt, underpants, and trousers, got dressed, returned to his office, and turned on the minifan.

"Catarella!"

"Comin', Chief."

He was closing the shutter when Catarella entered.

"Your ord . . ."

He trailed off, braced himself against the desk with his left hand, and brought his right hand to his forehead, closing his eyes. He looked like an illustration in a nineteenth-century acting manual for the expression "shock and dismay."

"Jesus, Jesus, Jesus . . ." he said in litany.

"Hey, Cat, you feel sick?"

"Jesus, Chief, whatta scare! The heat's got into my head!"

"But what's wrong?"

"Nuttin', Chief, go 'head 'n' talk, I feel fine. My ears are workin' great, iss my eyes got me seein' tings."

And he didn't move from his position: eyes shut tight, hand on his forehead.

"Listen, in the bathroom are some clothes I just changed out of—"

"Ya changed clothes?!" said Catarella.

He looked relieved, opened his eyes, lowered his hand from his forehead, and eyed Montalbano as if he'd never seen him before.

"So ya changed clothes!"

"Yeah, Cat, I changed clothes. What's so weird about that?"

"Nuttin' weird, Chief, it was juss a missunnerstannin! I seen ya come in dressed one ways 'n' then I seen ya dressed anutter ways 'n' so I tought I was loosinating cuzza the heat. 'Ssa good 'ting ya changed clothes!"

"Listen, go get those clothes and put them out in the courtyard to dry."

"I'll take care of it straightaways."

On his way out, he was about to close the door but the inspector stopped him.

"Leave it open, so there's a little draft."

The outside line rang. It was Mimì Augello.

"How are you doing, Salvo? I tried you at home but there was no answer, and then I remembered that you don't give a shit about August fifteenth, and so—"

"You were right, Mimì. How's Beba? And the kid?"

"Look, Salvo, don't even ask. You know what? The baby's

had a fever since the moment we got here! The upshot: We haven't managed to have a single day of vacation. Only yesterday did the fever pass, finally. And tomorrow I'm supposed to be back on the job . . ."

"I understand, Mimì. As far as I'm concerned, you can stay another week if you want."

"Really?"

"Really. Say hi to Beba for me and give your son a kiss."

Five minutes later, the other telephone rang.

"Aaahhh, Chief! Iss the c'mishner says he emergently needs to—"

"Tell him I'm not in."

"And where should I tell him you went to?"

"To the dentist's."

"You gotta toothache?"

"No, Cat, it's the excuse I want you to give him."

So the c'mishner was busting his balls even on August 15?

As he was signing some papers that Fazio explained had been piling up for a few months, he happened to look up. In the corridor he saw Catarella coming towards his office. But what was it that looked so strange about the way he was walking? The inspector knew the answer as soon as he asked the question.

Catarella, as he walked, was dancing. That was it. Dancing.

He was on tiptoe, arms stretched away from his body, hinting at a half pirouette every few steps. Had the heat indeed gone to his head? As he entered the office, the inspector noticed he was keeping his eyes closed. *O matre santa,* what had happened to him? Was he sleepwalking?

"Catarella!"

Catarella, who had come up to the desk, opened his eyes, stunned. He had a faraway look.

"Huh?" he said.

"What's got into you?"

"Ah, Chief, Chief! There's a girl here you gotta see with your eyes! She's the spittin' image of the poor girl that got killed! Mamma mia, she's so beautyfull! I never seen anyting like 'er."

It therefore was Beauty, with a capital B, that gave Catarella's step a dancing lilt, his gaze a dreamy look.

"Send her in and inform Fazio."

He saw her coming from the end of the corridor.

Catarella walked in front of her, literally bending forward, making a bizarre movement with his hand as if he were cleaning the ground in front of her where she was about to set foot. Or maybe he was unrolling an invisible carpet?

And as the girl approached and her features, eyes, and hair color became more and more distinct, the inspector slowly stood up, feeling himself happily drowning in a sort of blissful nothingness.

> *Head of pale gold*
> *With eyes of sky blue,*
> *Who gave you the power*
> *To make me no longer myself?*

It was a quatrain by Pessoa, singing in his head. He got hold of himself and emerged from the nothingness to return to his office.

But he had succeeded only by dealing himself a low, malicious blow as painful as it was necessary:

She could be your daughter.

"I'm Adriana Morreale."

"Salvo Montalbano's the name."

"Sorry I'm late, but . . ."

She was half an hour late.

They shook hands. The inspector's was a little sweaty, Adriana's was dry. She was all cool and fresh and smelled of soap, as if she wasn't coming in from outside but had just stepped out of the shower.

"Please sit down. Catarella, did you inform Fazio?"

"Huh?"

"Did you inform Fazio?"

"Straightaways, Chief."

He walked out with his head turned backwards, looking at the girl for as long as he could.

Montalbano took the opportunity to observe her, and she let herself be observed.

She must have been used to it.

Jeans clinging to very long legs, low-cut light blue blouse, sandals. One point in her favor: Her navel was not exposed. She was clearly not wearing a bra. And there wasn't a trace of makeup on her face. She did nothing to make herself beautiful. What more could she do, after all?

After a good look at her, one could see a few differences with respect to the photograph of her twin sister, due, no doubt, to the fact that Adriana was now six years older, and they mustn't have been easy years. The eyes had the same shape and color but the innocence that shone in Rina's gaze was gone from Adriana's. And the girl sitting in front of the inspector also had a very faint line at each corner of the mouth.

"Do you live with your parents in Vigàta?"

"No. I quickly realized that my presence was a painful reminder for them. They couldn't help but see my missing sister in me. So, when I enrolled at the university—I'm studying medicine—I bought an apartment in Palermo. But I come back often. I don't like to leave them alone for very long."

"What year of study are you in?"

"I've signed up for the third."

Fazio came in and, although he'd been prepared by Catarella, his eyes popped out the moment he saw her.

"Hi, my name's Fazio."

"I'm Adriana Morreale."

"Perhaps it's better if you shut the door," said the inspector.

Once news got around that a beautiful girl was in his office, in five minutes the hallway would be jammed with more traffic than a city street at rush hour.

Fazio closed the door and sat down in the other chair in front of the inspector's desk. But this brought him face-to-face with the girl. He decided to pull back until he was off to one side of the desk, slightly closer to Montalbano.

"Forgive me for not having you come to my place, Inspector."

"Not at all! I understand perfectly well."

"Thank you. You can go ahead and ask me all the questions you want."

"Prosecutor Tommaseo told us it was you who had to perform the painful task of identifying the body. I'm very sorry, but my job requires me, and I want to apologize right away for it, to ask you certain questions that—"

At this point Adriana did something that neither Fazio nor Montalbano were expecting. She threw her head back and started laughing.

"My God, you speak just like him! You and Tommaseo talk exactly the same way! Using the exact same words! Do they make you take some special course?"

Montalbano felt at once offended and liberated. Offended for having been compared to Tommaseo, and liberated because he realized the girl didn't like formalities. They made her laugh.

"I told you," Adriana continued, "to ask me all the questions you want. You don't have to walk on eggshells to do it. It doesn't really seem like your style."

"Thanks," said Montalbano.

Fazio, too, looked relieved.

"You, unlike your parents, always imagined your sister was dead, is that right?"

Just like that, cutting right to the quick, the way she wanted and the way everyone preferred.

Adriana gave him an admiring look.

"Yes, but I didn't imagine it. I knew it."

Montalbano and Fazio both, at the same time, leapt slightly out of their chairs.

"You *knew*? Who told you?"

"Nobody actually told me directly."

"So how did you know?"

"My body told me. And I've trained my body never to lie to me."

13

What did she mean by that?

"Could you please explain to me how . . ."

"It's not easy. It's because we were identical twins. The phenomenon is hard to explain, but it used to happen to us now and then. A sort of confused, long-distance communication of emotion."

"Could you explain that?"

"Sure. But first I want to make it clear that I'm not talking about the sort of phenomenon where if one of us skinned her knee, the other, even if she was far away, would feel pain in the same knee. Nothing like that. If anything, it was more like transmitting a strong emotion. One day, for example, Grandma died. Rina was there, but I was in Fela playing with my cousins, when, all of a sudden, I was overwhelmed by such a feeling of sadness that I started crying for no apparent reason. It was as though Rina had transmitted her emotions at that moment."

"Did this happen all the time?"

"No, not always."

"Where were you the day your sister didn't come home?"

"I'd left just that morning, on the twelfth, to see my aunt and uncle in Montelusa. I was supposed to stay with them for two or three days, but I came home late that same evening after Papa called my uncle to tell him Rina had disappeared."

"Listen ... on the afternoon, or the evening, of the twelfth ... was there anything ... you know ... any sort of 'communication,' between your sister and you ... ?"

Montalbano was having trouble formulating his question. Adriana helped him out.

"Yes, there was. At seven thirty-eight in the evening. I instinctively glanced at my watch."

Montalbano and Fazio looked at each other.

"What happened?"

"I had a little room of my own at my uncle and aunt's place, and I was alone, picking out clothes to wear that evening, because we'd been invited to dinner by some friends. All of a sudden I had this feeling, but not like the other times. It was sort of physical. She was strangled, wasn't she?"

She was close.

"Not exactly. What did Prosecutor Tommaseo tell you?"

"Prosecutor Tommaseo said that she'd been murdered, but he didn't specify how. He also told me where she'd been found."

"When you went to the morgue to identify the body—"

"I asked them to show me only the feet. That was enough. The big toe on her right—"

"I know. But afterward, didn't you ask Tommaseo how she died?"

"Listen, Inspector, my only concern after identifying the body was to liberate myself as quickly as possible from Tommaseo himself. He started to console me by patting me lightly on the back, but then his hand began sliding downwards, too far downwards. It's not really like me to play the prude—far from it—but that man was a real nuisance. What was he supposed to tell me?"

"That your sister had her throat slashed."

Adriana turned pale and brought her hand to her throat.

"Oh my God!" she whispered.

"Can you tell me what you felt at that moment?"

"A violent pain in my throat. For a minute that seemed like forever, I couldn't breathe. But at the time it didn't occur to me that the pain might be related to something that was happening to my sister."

"What did you think it was related to?"

"You see, Inspector, Rina and I were identical. But only physically. We were completely different in the way we thought, the way we acted. Rina, for example, would never have done anything against the rules, not even the slightest little thing, whereas I, on the other hand, would. In fact, I rather liked to, beginning around that time. So, for example, I started smoking on the sly. And that day I had smoked three cigarettes in a row, keeping the window in my little bedroom open. For no reason, just for the pleasure of doing it. So when I felt that pain in my throat, I naturally thought it was because of the cigarettes."

"And when did you realize that it had to do with your sister?"

"Immediately afterwards."

"Why?"

"I connected it to another thing that had happened to me just a few minutes earlier."

"Can you tell us what that was?"

"I'd rather not."

"Did you tell your parents about ... about this contact with your sister?"

"No. This is the first time I've talked about it."

"Why didn't you tell them?"

"Because it was a secret between Rina and me. We had sworn never to tell anyone."

"Did you and your sister confide a lot in each other?"

"How could we not?"

"Did you tell each other everything?"

"Everything."

Now came the most difficult questions.

"Would you like me to send for something from the café downstairs?"

"No, thanks. We can continue."

"Don't you have to go home? Are your parents alone?"

"Thanks, but please don't worry. I called a friend of mine to look after them. She's a nurse, so they're in good hands."

"Did Rina ever mention to you if there was anyone, during those final weeks, who was bothering her?"

Adriana did the same thing as before. She threw her head back and started laughing.

"Would you believe me, Inspector, if I told you there wasn't a single man, from age thirteen on up, who didn't 'bother' us, as you put it? I found it rather amusing, but Rina would feel bad about it, or else she would get very angry."

"There was one specific incident that was brought to our attention, and which we'd like to know more about."

"I know. You're talking about Ralf."

"You knew him?"

"It would have been hard not to. While his stepfather's house was being built, he would show up at our place every other day."

"What would he do?"

"Well, he would come and then he would hide, waiting for our parents to go into town or down to the beach. Then, after we got up, he would come and spy on us through the window as we were eating breakfast. I thought it was funny. Sometimes I would throw him little pieces of bread, as if he was a dog. He liked that little game. Rina couldn't stand him."

"Was he sane?"

"Are you kidding? He was out of his mind, totally. One day something more serious happened. I was alone in the house. The upstairs shower wasn't working. So I went and took a shower downstairs. When I came out, there he was, right in front of me, completely naked."

"How did he get inside?"

"Right through the front door. I had thought it was closed, but it had been left ajar. It was the first time Ralf came into the house. I didn't even have a towel around me. He looked at me with a doglike expression and asked me to give him a kiss."

"What did he say?"

"He said, 'Please, won't you give me a kiss?' "

"Weren't you afraid?"

"No. Those kinds of things don't frighten me."

"So, what was the upshot?"

"I figured it was best to give him what he wanted. So I kissed him. Very lightly, but on the lips. He put a hand on my breast and caressed it, then he bowed his head and collapsed in a chair. I ran upstairs and got dressed, and when I came back down he was gone."

"Didn't you think he might try to rape you?"

"Not even for a second."

"Why not?"

"Because I realized immediately that he was impotent. I could tell even from the way he looked at me. And I had my confirmation when I kissed him and he caressed me. He didn't have a, well, any visible reaction."

Deep inside his ears the inspector distinctly heard the sound of all his hypotheses falling noisily to pieces. Ralf forcing the girl to go into the underground apartment, raping her, killing her, and then killing himself or being forced to kill himself . . .

He exchanged a glance of dismay with Fazio, who looked befuddled himself.

Then he looked admiringly at Adriana. How many girls had he met who could say things so straightforwardly as she?

"Did you tell Rina about this incident?"

"Of course."

"So why did Rina run away when Ralf tried to kiss her? Didn't she know he was harmless?"

"Inspector, I already told you that as far as this sort of thing was concerned, we were very different. Rina wasn't afraid; she just felt deeply offended, and that's why she ran away."

"I was told that Spitaleri, the developer—"

"Yes, he happened to drive by in his car at that moment. He saw Rina running away and Ralf chasing after her, naked. He stopped, got out of his car, and punched Ralf so hard that he fell to the ground. Then he bent over him, pulled a knife out of his pocket, and told him that if he ever bothered my sister again, he would kill him."

"And then?"

"Then he had her get in his car and drove her home."

"Did he stay long?"

"Rina said she served him a cup of coffee."

"Do you know whether Spitaleri and your sister ever saw each other again?"

"Yes."

At that moment the telephone rang.

"Ah, Chief, Chief! The c'mishner wants to talk to you emergently straightaways and poissonally in poisson."

"But why didn't you tell him I was still at the dentist's?"

"I made an attemptation to tell 'im you's still out, but he said, the c'mishner said, I mean, not to tell 'im you's still at the dennist's and so I said you's here in the office in poisson."

"Put him on the line in Augello's office, and I'll pick up in there."

He stood up.

"You'll have to excuse me, Adriana. I'll be back as soon as I can. Fazio, you come with me."

In Mimì's office, with the sun shining straight in, the heat was stifling.

"Hello? What can I do for you, Mr. Commissioner?"

"Montalbano! Have you any idea?"

"Of what?"

"What? You don't have any idea?"

"Of what?"

"You didn't even deign to answer!"

"Answer what?"

"The questionnaire!"

"About what?"

Uttering any more syllables than that would have been painful.

"The questionnaire on personnel, which I sent you a good two weeks ago! It was extremely urgent!"

"It was filled out and sent."

"To me?!"

"Yes."

"When?"

"Six days ago."

A whopping lie.

"Did you make a copy?"

"Yes."

"If I can't find your answers, I'll let you know and you can send me the copy."

"Okay."

When he hung up, his shirt was dripping wet.

"Do you know anything about some questionnaire on personnel that the commissioner sent here about two weeks ago?" he asked Fazio.

"Yessir. I remember giving it to you."

"So where the hell did it end up? I have to find it and fill it out. The guy's liable to call back in half an hour. Let's go look for it."

"But the girl's still in your office."

"I'll have to send her home."

The girl was in the same position as when they'd left her. She seemed not to have budged.

"Listen, Adriana, something's come up. Can we meet again this afternoon?"

"I'm supposed to be home by five o'clock, when the nurse leaves."

"Can we make it tomorrow morning?"

"There's the funeral."

"Well, then, I don't know . . ."

"I've got an idea. I invite you both to lunch. That way, we can continue talking. If you feel like it . . ."

"Thank you very much," said Fazio, "but I have to go home. It's August fifteenth, after all."

"I, on the other hand, would be delighted to come," said Montalbano. "Where will you take me?"

"Wherever you like."

Montalbano couldn't believe it. They made an appointment to meet at Enzo's at one-thirty.

"That girl's got balls of steel," Fazio muttered as she went out.

Left alone, Montalbano and Fazio searched all over the room and got discouraged. The desk was completely covered with papers, and there were stacks of paper on the caddy with water and glasses, on top of the file cabinet, and even on the little sofa and the two armchairs for important visitors.

They worked up a royal sweat and took a good half hour to find the questionnaire. But the worst was yet to come, and they sweated even more filling in the answers.

When they had finished, it was past one o'clock. Fazio said good-bye and left.

"Catarella!"

"Here I am."

"Photocopy these four pages for me. Then, if anyone from the commissioner's office should call asking about a questionnaire, send them the photocopy you've made. But be absolutely certain: the photocopy!"

"Don' worry, Chief."

"Now, go get the clothes you set out to dry and bring them to me. Then go and open the doors to my car."

Undressing in the bathroom, he had the impression that his skin stank. It must have been all the effort he'd made searching for that goddamned questionnaire. He washed himself thoroughly, changed clothes, gave Catarella the sweaty clothes to put in the courtyard, and went into Augello's office. He knew that Mimì kept a little bottle of cologne in one of his drawers. He looked for it and found it. It was called *Irresistible*. He unscrewed the cap and, thinking that there was a dropper, managed to empty half the bottle on his shirt and pants. Now what? Should he put the sweaty clothes back on? No, maybe out in the open air the cologne would evaporate. Then he had a moment of hesitation: Should he bring the minifan or not? He decided against it. He would surely have looked ridiculous to Adriana, holding the little contraption to his face and smelling sweet as a whore.

Despite the fact that he'd had Catarella open the doors, getting inside the car was like entering a furnace. But he didn't feel up to walking all the way to Enzo's, especially as he was already late.

In front of the trattoria, which was closed, Adriana stood in the scorching sun, beside a Fiat Punto. He'd forgotten that Enzo celebrated the August 15 holiday by closing the restaurant.

"Follow me," he said to the girl.

Near the bar in Marinella there was a trattoria he'd never tried. But, driving by in his car, he'd noticed that the tables outside were always in shade, protected by a very dense pergola. It took them ten minutes to get there. Despite the holiday, there weren't many people at the restaurant, and they were able to choose a table more isolated than the rest.

"Did you change and douse yourself with cologne for my sake?" Adriana asked mischievously.

"No, for my own sake. As for the cologne, the bottle spilled all over me," he said gravely.

He probably would have been better off smelling of sweat.

They sat there in silence until the waiter appeared and started reciting the litany.

"An' we got spaghetti wit' tomata sauce, spaghetti in squid ink, spaghetti wit' sea urchin, spaghetti wit' clam sauce, spaghetti—"

"I'll have it with the clam sauce," Montalbano interrupted him. "And you?"

"With sea urchin."

The waiter then began a different litany.

"For seconds we got salt-baked mullet, baked gilthead, sea bass in sauce, grilled turbot—"

"You can tell us later," said Montalbano.

The waiter looked offended. He returned a few minutes later with cutlery, glasses, water, and wine, white and ice-cold.

"Would you like some?"

"Yes."

Montalbano poured her half a glass and did the same for himself.

"It's good," she said.

"Would you believe I can't remember where we left off?"

"You were asking me if Spitaleri and Rina had crossed paths on any other occasion, and I said yes."

"Ah, yes, right. What did your sister say about that?"

"She said that after that time with Ralf, Spitaleri started hovering over her a bit too much."

"In what sense?"

"Rina had the impression that Spitaleri was spying on her. She would run into him a little too often. For example, if she took the bus into town, on the way back Spitaleri would appear and offer her a lift home. And this, up until a week before."

"A week before what?"

"Before the twelfth of October."

"And Rina would let him drive her home?"

"Sometimes."

"And did Spitaleri always behave?"

"Yes."

"And what happened a week before your sister disappeared?"

"Something unpleasant. That evening, it was already dark, and Rina accepted the ride. But right after they turned onto the little road for Pizzo, in front of the house that belongs to that peasant who was later arrested, Spitaleri stopped the car and started putting his hands all over her. Just like that, out the blue, according to Rina."

"What did your sister do?"

"She screamed so loudly that the peasant came running out of his house. Rina saw her chance and took refuge in the man's house. Spitaleri was forced to leave."

"How did Rina go home?"

"On foot. The peasant walked her home."

"You said he was arrested?"

"Yes, poor thing. When police began looking for her, they searched his house as well. And, as luck would have it, they found one of my sister's earrings under some furniture. Rina thought it had fallen in Spitaleri's car, whereas in fact she'd lost it there. And so I decided to tell the police what had happened with Spitaleri. But it was useless. You know how the police are, don't you?"

"Yes, I do."

"The poor man was persecuted for months."

"Do you know if they questioned Spitaleri?"

"Of course. But Spitaleri told them that on the morning of the twelfth he'd left for Bangkok. It couldn't have been him."

The waiter arrived with the spaghetti.

Adriana brought the first forkful to her mouth, tasted it, then said:

"It's good. Would you like to try some?"

"Why not?"

Montalbano reached over, armed with a fork, and rolled the spaghetti onto it. The food wasn't comparable to Enzo's, but it was edible enough.

"You try mine."

Adriana did the same as him and tasted.

They didn't speak again until they had finished. Every now and then they looked at each other and smiled.

Something strange had occurred. It was as if the familiarity of sticking one's fork into the other's dish had established a sort of mutual confidence, an intimacy, that hadn't existed before.

14

They had finished eating for some time but still weren't talking. As they each sipped a cold, digestive limoncello, Montalbano could feel her observing him, just as he had observed her at the station. Just to appear nonchalant—since it was hard to pretend nothing was happening, with those eyes the color of the sea looking at him—he fired up a cigarette.

"Could I have one, too, please?"

He held out the pack, she extracted a cigarette, put it between her lips, and half stood up, bending far forward to light it from the inspector's lighter.

Don't forget she could be your daughter! the inspector admonished himself.

What he was seeing, thanks to the girl's position, made his head start spinning wildly. And the skin under his mustache became wet with sweat.

There was no way she didn't know that by leaning forward in that manner, he would be forced to look down her blouse. So why had she done it? To provoke him? But Adriana didn't seem the type to resort to such manipulations.

Or had she done it because she thought he had already

reached an age where one no longer paid much attention to women? Yes, that must be it.

He didn't have time to start feeling sorry for himself before the girl, after taking two puffs, suddenly put her hand on top of his.

Since Adriana showed no sign of feeling the heat—in fact, she looked fresh as a proverbial daisy—the inspector was amazed to find that she had such a burning touch. Was it the combination of their body heat, his and hers, that made the temperature increase? And, if not, just how hot was the blood circulating inside her?

"She was raped, wasn't she?"

It was the question that Montalbano, at every moment, had been expecting, fearing. He had prepared a good, articulate answer in advance, which he now completely forgot.

"No," he said.

Why did he answer that way? So as not to see the light of beauty go out before him?

"You're not telling me the truth."

"Believe me, Adriana, the autopsy revealed that—"

"That she was a virgin?"

"Yes."

"That's even worse," she said.

"Why?"

"Because in that case the violence was even more horrific."

The pressure from her hand, which was now scalding hot, increased.

"Could we drop the formalities?"

"If you like . . ."

"I want to tell you something in all confidence."

She let go of his hand, which suddenly felt cold, stood up, grabbed her chair, put it next to Montalbano's, and sat down. Now she could speak softly, whisper.

"She most certainly was raped, I'm sure of it. When we were at the station I didn't want to tell you in front of that other man. But with you, it's different."

"You mentioned that a few minutes before feeling the pain in your throat, you'd felt something else."

"Yes. A sense of total, utter panic. A terror, a sort of fear for my very existence. It had never happened to me before."

"Try and explain it to me."

"All of a sudden, as I was standing near the armoire, I saw my sister's image reflected in the mirror. She was upset, terrified. One second later I felt myself plunged into total darkness. Horrifying. It was as if I was enveloped in something slimy, without light or air, something malignant. A place—well, not really a place, but where every sort of horror or outrage became possible. Like what happens in nightmares. I wanted to scream, but my voice made no sound. I also know that I went blind for a few seconds. I groped around in the emptiness and then leaned against a wall so I wouldn't fall. And that was when . . ."

She stopped. Montalbano didn't say a word, didn't move. Sweat started dripping down his forehead.

"That was when I felt robbed."

"How?" the inspector couldn't help but ask.

"Robbed of myself. It's hard to put into words. Someone was violently, ferociously taking possession of my body, separating it from me, to offend it, humiliate it, annihilate it, to make it an object, a thing ..."

Her voice cracked.

"That's enough," said Montalbano.

And he took her hands in his.

"Is that what happened?" she asked.

"We think so."

But why wasn't she crying? Her eyes had turned a darker blue, the wrinkle at the corners of her mouth had deepened, but she wasn't crying.

What was it that gave her such strength, such inner toughness? Was it perhaps the fact that she knew that Rina had died at the very moment she was killed, whereas her mother and father had kept on hoping that their daughter was still alive?

Perhaps after all these years, the pain, the sorrow, the tears had clotted into a kind of solid mass, a stony lump that would never again dissolve into an expression of pity for Rina or herself.

"A minute ago you said you saw your sister's image in the mirror. What did you mean?"

She smiled ever so slightly.

"It all began as a game when we were five years old. We would stand in front of the mirror and start talking. But not directly. We would each turn towards the other's reflection.

We kept on doing it, even after we grew up. When we had something really serious or secret to tell, we would go stand in front of the mirror."

The girl then rested her head on Montalbano's shoulder for a moment. He realized that it was not to seek comfort, but to alleviate the profound weariness she must have felt from speaking to a stranger about something so intimate, so secret.

Then she stood up decisively and looked at her watch.

"It's already three-thirty. Shall we go?"

"If you want."

But hadn't she said she could stay out until five?

Montalbano got up, feeling slightly disappointed, and the waiter prepared the check.

"Let me pay for this," said Adriana.

And she pulled some money out of the pocket of her jeans.

But when they were in the parking lot, she made no move towards her car. Montalbano gave her a puzzled look.

"Let's take yours," she said.

"Where to?"

"If you've understood me, you've also understood where I want to go. I don't need to tell you."

He had, of course, understood. He'd understood perfectly well. But he was acting like the soldier who doesn't want to go to war.

"Do you think it's appropriate?"

She didn't answer, but only kept looking at him.

Montalbano realized that in the end he would not be

able to say no to her. The soldier would go to war, there were no two ways about it. And anyway, the sun was beating down on them like a sledgehammer there in the parking lot. It was impossible to remain out in the open one moment longer.

"All right, get in."

Getting into the car was like lying down on a grill.

Montalbano regretted not bringing his minifan. Adriana opened all the windows.

For the duration of the drive, she sat with her head leaning out the window, eyes closed.

The inspector, on the other hand, had a nagging question boring into his brain: Wasn't he doing something incredibly stupid? Why had he agreed to go along? Just because the heat in the parking lot made it impossible to discuss things? But that was only the excuse he'd come up with on the spot. The truth was that he rather liked helping this girl, who—

Who could be your own daughter! his conscience interrupted.

You stay out of this! Montalbano replied angrily. *I was thinking of something entirely different, that is, that this poor girl has been carrying a terrible weight inside her for six years, the exact intuition of what happened to her sister, and only now is she finding the strength to talk about it and unburden herself. It's only right to help her.*

You're just a hypocrite, worse than Tommaseo, said the voice of his conscience.

As soon as they turned onto the dirt road to Pizzo, Adriana opened her eyes.

When they were passing in front of her house, the girl said:

"Stop!"

She didn't get out, but only looked at the house from the car.

"We've never gone back since then. I know that from time to time Papa sends a woman over to clean it and keep it in order, but we just haven't had the courage to come back here in the summer, like we used to do . . . Okay, we can go now."

When Montalbano pulled up in front of the last house, the girl was already opening the car door.

"Do you really have to do this, Adriana?"

"Yes."

He left the car open, the keys in the ignition. In any case, there was not a living soul around.

Once out of the car, Adriana took his hand and brought it to her lips, resting them there for a moment, then continued holding it tightly. He led her to the side of the house where one could enter the illegal apartment. Forensics had placed two planks there to facilitate descent. The window to the small bathroom was covered with ribbons of colored plastic of the sort used for road work. From one of these strips dangled a sheet of paper with stamps and signatures. It was the official seal. The inspector removed it all and went in first, telling the girl to wait for him. He turned on the flashlight he'd brought with him and checked all the rooms. The few minutes it took to walk around the apartment sufficed to drench him in sweat. There was a sort of viscous humidity in those underground rooms, and it felt grimy, dirty; the stale, heavy air burned the eyes and throat.

He went back and helped the girl climb through the window.

Once inside, Adriana took the flashlight from him and started walking, heading straight for the living room.

As if she'd been there before, the inspector thought, bewildered, as he followed her.

Adriana then stopped in the doorway to the living room and shone the flashlight's beam on the walls, the pile of frames wrapped in plastic, and the trunk. She acted as if she'd forgotten that Montalbano was beside her. She said nothing, but was breathing heavily.

"Adriana . . ."

The girl didn't hear him, but only continued her personal descent into hell.

She started walking, but slowly, as though uncertain. She turned slightly to the left, towards the trunk, then turned again to the right, took three steps, and stopped.

As she was moving about in this manner, Montalbano, who ended up almost in front of her, noticed she had her eyes closed. She was looking for an exact spot, not with her eyes, but with some other, unknown sense that she alone must have possessed.

Having arrived to the left of the French door, she placed her hands on the wall as though bracing herself, her legs spread apart.

"*Matre santa!*" Montalbano said in terror.

Was he witnessing a sort of reenactment of what had happened in that room? Was Adriana perhaps possessed by Rina's spirit?

All at once the flashlight fell to the floor. Luckily it didn't go out.

Adriana was standing in the exact same spot where Forensics had placed the pool of blood. Her body was shaking all over.

It's not possible, it's not possible! Montalbano said to himself. His rational mind refused to believe what he saw.

Then he heard a sound that paralyzed him. Not weeping, but a kind of wail. Like a mortally wounded animal's wail, long, sustained, soft. It was coming from Adriana.

Montalbano sprang, bent down, picked up the flashlight, grabbed the girl by the hips and pulled. But she resisted. It was as though her hands were glued to the wall. The inspector then worked his way between her arms and the wall, shot the beam of the flashlight in her face, but the girl still had her eyes closed.

From her twisted, half-open mouth came the distressing wail, and now there was a thread of drool as well. Dismayed, he slapped her hard twice, with the front and the back of his hand.

Adriana reopened her eyes, looked at him, and embraced him with all her might, pressing her body firmly against him and pushing him up against the wall. Then she kissed him hard, biting his lips. Montalbano felt the ground go out from under his feet and grabbed on to her as if not to fall, as her kiss went on and on.

Then the girl let go, turned, ran to the bathroom window, and climbed through it. Montalbano followed fast behind her, having no time to put the seals back up.

Racing to Montalbano's car, Adriana got into the driver's seat and turned on the ignition. Montalbano barely managed in time to get in on the other side as the car was pulling away.

Adriana then stopped the car in front of her house, got out, ran to the door, searched in her pockets, found the key, opened the door, and went in, leaving it open behind her.

By the time Montalbano was inside, she was gone.

What should he do now? He heard her vomiting somewhere.

He went outside and slowly walked around the house. The silence was total. Except for the thousands of cicadas, that is. At one time there must have been a field of wheat behind the house, because he saw a *pagliaro* there, a tall, narrow hut made of straw and agave flowers.

Under a clump of long-yellowed weeds, a sparrow was rolling around in the dry dirt, cleaning itself in the absence of water.

He felt like doing the same. He, too, needed to clean himself, of all the filth that had stuck to his skin when he was in the underground apartment.

Then, without realizing what he was doing, he did something he used to do as a little boy. He took off his shirt, pants, and underwear, and, completely naked, pressed his body against the *pagliaro*.

Then he opened his arms as wide as he could and embraced the hut, trying to stick his head as far inside as possible. He was forcing his way into the *pagliaro*, thrusting all of his body weight forward, moving it first to the right, then to the left. And when, at last, he began to smell the clean, dry odor of withered straw, he breathed it in deep, and deeper still, until he detected a scent that surely existed only in his imagination, that of the sea breeze, which had managed to wend its way into the dense web of dried stalks and remain trapped therein. A sea breeze with a slightly bitter aftertaste, as if burnt by the August heat.

All at once, half the *pagliaro* collapsed on top of him, covering him up.

He stayed that way, immobile, feeling cleansed by every blade of straw that had come to rest on his skin.

Once, as a child, he had done the exact same thing, and his aunt, no longer seeing him anywhere, had started to call to him.

"Salvo! Where are you? Salvo?"

But that wasn't his aunt's voice—that was Adriana calling him, just a few yards away!

He felt lost. He could not let her see him naked. What the hell had got into him? Why had he gone and done such a silly thing? Was he insane? Was it the intense heat that was making him fuck up so much? How was he going to find a way out of this ridiculous situation?

"Salvo? Where are you? Sal . . ."

Surely she had just spotted his clothes on the ground! He realized she was drawing closer.

She'd found him. *Matre santa,* how embarrassing! He closed his eyes, hoping to become invisible. He heard her laughing wildly, surely throwing back her beautiful head as she had done at the station. His heart started pounding with increased pressure. Now *that* was an idea: Why couldn't he have a nice little heart attack? Then, more strongly than the scent of withered straw, more strongly than the sea breeze, he smelled the overwhelming fragrance of her clean skin. She had taken a shower. The girl must now have been only inches away.

"If you stick out your arm, I'll hand you your things," said Adriana.

Montalbano obeyed.

"Okay, don't worry, I'm turning my back now," the girl continued.

The only problem was that she kept laughing, humiliating him, the whole time he was clumsily getting dressed.

"I'm late," Adriana said as they were getting into the car. "Would you let me drive?"

She had realized that, when it came to driving fast, Montalbano was a lost cause.

For the entire ride—which was over quickly, with them pulling up in the restaurant's parking lot in the twinkling of an eye—she kept her right hand on his knee, driving with only her left. Was it this way of driving or the heat that left the inspector bathed in sweat?

"Are you married?"

"No."

"Do you have a girlfriend?"

"Yes, but she doesn't live in Vigàta."

Why had he blurted that out?

"What's her name?"

"Livia."

"Where do you live?"

"In Marinella."

"Give me your home phone number."

Montalbano said it, and she repeated it.

"Already memorized."

They arrived. The inspector got out of the car. She too. They found themselves standing one in front of the other. Adriana put her hands on his hips and kissed him lightly.

"Thanks," she said.

The inspector watched her drive away, tires screeching.

He decided not to drop in at the station but to go directly home. It was almost six o'clock when, dressed in his bathing suit, he opened the French door giving onto the veranda. And there he found three youngsters sitting down, two boys and a girl, each about twenty. It was clear they had made his veranda their home for the entire day; they had eaten, drunk, and taken off their clothes to go swimming there. There were still dozens of people on the beach, taking in the sun's last rays.

But scattered all across the sand were scraps of paper, leftovers, empty boxes and bottles. In short, a veritable dump. The veranda, too, had been turned into a dump, the deck scattered with a hodgepodge of cigarette butts and roaches, cans of beer and Coca-Cola.

"Before you leave, I want you to clean all this up," he

said, descending the short flight of steps and heading towards the water.

"Okay, but you clean your asshole first," said one of the boys behind him.

The other two started laughing.

He could have just ignored it, but he turned around instead and slowly approached them.

"Who said that?"

"Me," said the huskier of the two guys in an arrogant tone.

"Come down here."

The kid looked at his friends.

"Let's go help the old man. I'll be right back."

The kid plunked himself in front of him with legs spread, then reached out and shoved him twice.

"Go take your swim, Grandpa."

Montalbano started him out with a left, which the kid dodged, while his right, as planned, got him square in the face and dropped him straight to the ground, half unconscious. It wasn't so much a punch as a wallop. The other two quickly stopped laughing.

"When I get back, I want it all cleaned up."

He had to swim out a ways to find a bit of clean water, since closer to shore there was all manner of foreign objects, from turds to plastic cups, floating on the surface. A pigsty.

Before going back, he looked shoreward, searching for a spot where there were fewer people and therefore the water was probably less filthy. This meant, however, that he had to walk for half an hour on the beach to get back to his house.

The kids were gone. And the veranda was clean.

In the shower, which was still warm, he thought of the punch that had half knocked the kid out. How could he possibly be still capable of such strength? Then he realized it wasn't only a question of strength, but also of the violent release of all the tension he had built up inside him on that August 15.

15

Late that evening, the families with little kids crying one minute and screaming the next, the drunken, brawling parties of friends, the young couples stuck so tightly together that you couldn't have separated them with a knife, the solitary males with cell phones glued to their ears, the other young couples with radios, CD players, and other noisemaking gadgets finally vacated the beach.

They went away, but their garbage remained.

Garbage, the inspector thought, had become the unmistakable sign that man had passed through any given place. In fact, they say Mount Everest has become a trash heap and that even outer space is a dump.

Ten thousand years from now, the sole proof that man once lived on this earth will be the discovery of enormous car cemeteries, the only surviving monument of a former, ahem, civilization.

After he'd been sitting awhile on the veranda, he began to notice that the air stank. The garbage covering the beach was no longer visible in the darkness, yet the stench of rapid putrefaction from the extreme heat still wafted up to his nostrils.

There was no point in remaining outside. But neither was it possible to stay inside with all the windows closed to keep out the stink, because the heat that the walls had absorbed during the day would never have a chance to dispel.

So he got dressed, took the car, and headed off in the direction of Pizzo. Arriving at the house, he pulled up, got out, and headed towards the staircase that led down to the beach.

He sat down on the first step and lit a cigarette. He'd been right. The spot was too high up to be affected by the smell of rot from the garbage that must surely lie scattered across that beach, too.

He tried not to think of Adriana, but didn't succeed.

He stayed that way for two hours, and by the time he got up to go back home, he had come to the conclusion that the less he saw of the girl, the better.

"So what did Miss Adriana tell you yesterday?" Fazio asked.

"She told me something I didn't know for certain but had imagined. Do you remember when Dipasquale told us, and Adriana confirmed, that Rina had been assaulted by Ralf and that Spitaleri had saved her?"

"Of course I remember."

The inspector then recounted the whole story of how from that moment on Spitaleri had been constantly after Rina until he finally groped her in his car, and the girl was saved when a peasant appeared on the scene. And he also mentioned how the peasant had been run through the gauntlet by police when one of Adriana's earrings was found in his house even though the poor guy had nothing to do with the crime.

He said not a word about the fact that he had gone back to the house in Pizzo with Adriana or about what had happened there.

"In conclusion," said Fazio, "we've got nothing to work with. It can't have been Ralf, because he was impotent, it can't have been Spitaleri because he was gone, and it can't have been Dipasquale because he's got an alibi . . ."

"Dipasquale's position is the weakest," said the inspector. "His alibi may have been made up."

"Yeah, but try and prove that."

"Chief, iss Porxecutor Dommaseo."

"Put 'im on."

"Montalbano? I've made a decision."

"Tell me."

"I'm going to do it."

And he's telling *him* about it?

"You're going to do what?"

"Hold a press conference."

"But what need is there?"

"Oh, there's need, Montalbano, there's need!"

The only need was Tommaseo's need to appear on television.

"The newsmen," the prosecutor continued, "have gotten wind of something and are starting to ask questions. I don't want to run the risk of them giving a distorted image of the overall picture."

What overall picture?

"It's true that's a pretty big risk."

"So you agree?"

"Have you already set it up?"

"Yes, for tomorrow morning at eleven. Will you be there?"

"No. And what will you say?"

"I'll talk about the crime."

"Will you say she was raped?"

"Well, I'll suggest it."

Great! It took less than a suggestion to have the journalists jump all over that sort of subject!

"And what if they ask if you have any idea as to the murderer?"

"Well, one has to be adroit in these situations."

"As you are."

"In all modesty . . . I'll say that we're following two leads: The first is that we're checking on the alibis of the masons, and the second is that we're investigating a maniac drifter who forced the girl to go with him into the underground apartment. Are you in agreement?"

"Perfectly."

A maniac drifter! And how would a maniac drifter have known about the secret illegal apartment if the construction site was fenced off?

"For today, I've called Adriana back in for questioning," Tommaseo said. "I want to break down any residual defenses she may have, to interrogate her thoroughly—thoroughly and at great length, to lay her completely bare."

His voice had turned shrill. Montalbano was afraid that, two more words and the guy would have started moaning and saying *ah, ah, ah,* just like in a porn flick.

It was already becoming a habit. Before going to Enzo's trattoria, he changed his clothes and gave the sweaty ones to Catarella. Then, after eating—though he ate little, having almost no appetite—he felt sort of listless and decided to go home to Marinella.

Miracle of miracles! Four garbage collectors had nearly finished cleaning the beach! He put on his bathing suit and dived into the sea in search of relief from the heat. Afterwards he dozed off for an hour.

By four o'clock he was back at the station. But he didn't feel like doing anything.

"Catarella!"

"Whattya need, Chief?"

"Don't let anyone into my office without alerting me first, is that clear?"

"Yessir."

"Oh, and, did anyone call from Montelusa about the questionnaire?"

"Yessir, Chief, I sennit over to 'em."

He locked the door to his room, stripped down to his

underpants, threw the papers that were on the armchair onto the floor, pulled it up next to the minifan, which he turned in such a way that it blew onto his chest, and then sat down, hoping to survive.

An hour later the telephone rang.

"Chief, iss a marshal called La Caña says 'e's wit' da Finance Police."

"Put him on."

"I can't put 'im on, seeing as how the beforementioned marshal is 'ere poissonally in poisson."

God, and he was practically naked!

"Tell him I'm on the phone, wait five minutes, then let him in."

He got dressed in a hurry. His clothes were exactly the same as when he'd just stretched them out to dry, still saturated with heat. He opened the door and went out to meet Laganà, brought him into the office, sat him down, and locked the door. He felt embarrassed to find the marshal dressed in a suit that looked like he'd just picked it up from the cleaners.

"Would you like anything to drink, Marshal?"

"No thanks, Inspector. Whatever I drink only makes me sweat."

"Why'd you put yourself out? You could have phoned—"

"Inspector, nowadays it's better not to say certain things over the phone."

"Maybe we ought to use little folded-up pieces of paper, like Provenzano."

"They'd probably get intercepted, too. The only way is to talk in person and, if possible, in a safe place."

"I think it's safe here."

"Let's hope so."

The marshal slipped a hand into his jacket pocket, extracted a sheet of paper folded in four, and handed it to Montalbano.

"Is this what you were interested in?"

It was the receipt from Ribaudo Enterprises for some innocent pipes and some safety railings, delivered on July 27 to the Spitaleri construction site in Montelusa. It was signed by Filiberto Attanasio, the watchman.

Montalbano felt heartened.

"Thank you, this is exactly what I was looking for. Did anyone notice?"

"I don't think so. This morning we seized two crates of documents. As soon as I found that receipt, I had it photocopied and brought it here to you."

"I don't know how to thank you."

Marshal Laganà stood up. So did Montalbano.

"I'll see you out."

As they were shaking hands in the main entrance to the station, Laganà said with a smile:

"There's no point in my insisting that you say nothing to anyone about how that document was obtained."

"Marshal, you're offending me."

Laganà hesistated a moment, turned serious, and then said in a low voice:

"Be careful how you deal with Spitaleri."

"Federico? Montalbano here."

Inspector Lozupone seemed truly happy to hear from him.

"Salvo! What a pleasant surprise! How are you?"

"Fine. And you?"

"Fine, thanks. Do you need anything?"

"I'd like to speak with you."

"Sure, go ahead."

"In person."

"Is it urgent?"

"Fairly."

"Look, I'll definitely be in my office until—"

"Better outside somewhere."

"Ah. We could meet at the Caffè Marino at—"

"Not in public."

"You're starting to frighten me, Salvo. Where, then?"

"Either at my place or yours."

"I have a curious wife."

"Then come to my house in Marinella. You know where it is. Ten o'clock tonight okay with you?"

At eight, as the inspector was leaving the office, Tommaseo called. He sounded disappointed.

"I want a confirmation from you."

"I confirm."

"Excuse me, Montalbano, but what are you confirming?"

"Ah, well, I don't know what, but if you're asking me for a confirmation, I'm ready to give you one."

"Even if you don't know what you're supposed to confirm?"

"I see, you don't want a generic confirmation, but a specific one."

"I'd say so!"

Every now and then he liked to fuck with Tommaseo's head.

"Then tell me what it is."

"That girl, Adriana, today . . . among other things, she was even more beautiful. I don't know how she does it; she's like the essence of woman. Whatever she says, whatever she does, one is left utterly charmed and . . . ah, never mind, what was I saying?"

"That one is left utterly charmed."

"My God, no, I was just saying that incidentally. Ah, yes, Adriana told me her sister had once been assaulted, luckily without consequences, by a young German who later died in a railway disaster in Germany. I'm going to mention this at the press conference."

Railway disaster? What the hell had Tommaseo understood?

"But no matter how much pressure I put on her," the prosecutor continued, "she couldn't or wouldn't tell me any

more, claiming that it was pointless for me to continue inter-
rogating her, since she and her twin sister never confided in
each other and, she added, often quarreled so violently that
their parents did all they could to keep them apart. In fact,
the day Rina was murdered, Adriana wasn't even in Vigàta.
So, since the girl told me you questioned her yesterday, my
question to you is, did she also tell you she didn't get along
with her sister?"

"Absolutely! She said they even came to blows two or
three times a day."

"So it's pointless to call her in for further questioning?"

"I'm afraid so."

Obviously Adriana got sick and tired of Tommaseo and
made up that lie, knowing she could count on the inspector's
complicity.

Adriana phoned him at home around nine that evening.

"Can I drop by in about an hour?"

"I'm sorry, but I have an engagement."

And if he hadn't, what would he have answered?

"Too bad. I wanted to take advantage of the fact that my
aunt and uncle are here from Milan. I told you about them;
they were the ones who lived in Montelusa."

"Yes, I remember."

"They came down for the funeral."

He'd completely forgotten about it.

"When is it?"

"Tomorrow morning. They're leaving immediately afterwards. Don't make any engagements for tomorrow evening; I'm hoping my nurse friend can come."

"Adriana, I have a job that—"

"Try to do your best. Oh, Tommaseo called me in for questioning today. He was positively drooling as he stared at my tits. And to think that I'd put on a reinforced bra for the occasion. I told him a lie, just to get him out of my hair, once and for all."

"I know what you told him. He phoned me to ask if it was true that you and Rina couldn't stand each other."

"What did you say?"

"I confirmed it."

"I knew I could count on you. I love you. See you tomorrow."

He ran into the bathroom and got into the shower before Lozupone arrived. Those three words, *I love you,* had immediately made him break out in a drenching sweat.

Lozupone was five years his junior, a man of powerful build and pithy speech. Not the sort to set tongues wagging, he was honest and had always done his duty. Montalbano, therefore, had to proceed carefully with him and choose the right words. He offered him a whisky and sat him down on the veranda. Luckily a light wind was blowing.

"Salvo, get to the point. What do you have to tell me?"

"It's a delicate matter, and before making any moves, I want to talk to you about it."

"Here I am."

"These days I've been busy working on the homicide of a girl ..."

"Yes, I've heard mention of it."

"And I happened to interrogate a builder named Spitaleri, whom you also know."

Lozupone seemed to react defensively.

"What do you mean, I know him? I only know him because I investigated the accidental death of a mason at one of his construction sites in Montelusa."

"That's just it. I wanted to know more about this investigation of yours. What conclusion did you come to?"

"I think I just said it a second ago: accidental death. The worksite, when I went there, was up to code. I had it reopened after it had been shut down for five days. Laurentano, the prosecutor, was pressing me to hurry up."

"When were you first called?"

"On a Monday morning, after the mason's body was found. And I repeat, all the safety measures were in order. The only possible conclusion was that the Arab, who'd had a bit too much to drink, climbed over the protective railing and fell. And, in fact, the autopsy showed that there was more wine than blood in his body."

Montalbano balked, but didn't let Lozupone see. If things had really happened the way Lozupone said and Spitaleri maintained, then why had Filiberto told a different story? Most importantly, wasn't there the receipt from Ribaudo's proving that the watchman was telling the truth? Wasn't it better to shoot straight with Lozupone and tell him what he, Montalbano, thought about the matter?

"Federì, didn't it ever occur to you that maybe, when the mason fell, there wasn't any protection and that the railing was put up on Sunday? So that, when you came on Monday morning, everything would be in order?"

Lozupone refilled his glass with whisky.

"Of course it occurred to me," he said.

"And what did you do?"

"What you yourself would have done."

"Namely?"

"I asked Spitaleri what firm supplied him with his scaffolding. And he said Ribaudo's. So I reported this to Laurentano. I wanted him to question Ribaudo, or to authorize me to question Ribaudo. But he said no. He said that for him, the investigation ended there."

"Well, the proof you were looking for from Ribaudo I managed to procure myself. Spitaleri had the materials sent that Sunday at dawn, and he assembled it with the help of the worksite foreman Dipasquale and the watchman Attanasio."

"And what do you intend to do with this proof?"

"Give it either to you or to Prosecutor Laurentano."

"Let me see it."

Montalbano handed him the receipt. Lozupone looked at it and handed it back.

"This doesn't prove anything."

"Didn't you see the date? July the twenty-seventh was a Sunday!"

"You know what Laurentano might say to you? First, that given the ongoing working relationship between Spitaleri and Ribaudo, it wasn't the first time Ribaudo furnished materials to Spitaleri on a Sunday. Second, that the material was needed because on Monday morning, they were supposed to begin construction on several new floors of the building. Third: Would you please explain to me, Inspector Montalbano, how you happened to get your hands on this document? To conclude, Spitaleri gets off and you, and whoever gave you the document, take it up the ass."

"But is Laurentano in on this?"

"Laurentano?! What are you saying? Laurentano only wants to advance his career. And if you're going to get ahead, rule number one is to let sleeping dogs lie."

Montalbano felt so enraged that he blurted out:

"And what does your father-in-law Lattes think about it?"

"Lattes? Don't stray too far, Salvo. Don't piss outside the urinal. My father-in-law has certain political interests, it's true, but he's certainly never said anything to me about this Spitaleri business."

Go figure why, Montalbano felt satisfied with this answer.

"And so you surrender?"

"What, in your opinion, should I do? Start tilting at windmills like Don Quixote?"

"Spitaleri is not a windmill."

"Montalbà, let's be frank. Do you know why Laurentano doesn't want to let me go any further? Because when he puts Spitaleri and his political protectors on one side of his personal scale, and the dead body of an anonymous Arab immigrant on the other, which way do you think the scale tips?

The death of the Arab was given three lines of coverage in only one newspaper. What do you think will happen if we go after Spitaleri? A pandemonium of television, radio, newspapers, interpellations in parliament, pressure, maybe even blackmail. And so I ask you: How many people, among us and among the judges, have the same scale in their offices as Laurentano?"

16

He felt so furious that he stayed out on the veranda to finish the bottle of whisky, specifically intending, if not to get drunk, then at least to numb himself enough to be able to go to bed.

After thinking it over, with a cool head and without getting too carried away, he realized Lozupone was right. He would never succeed in screwing Spitaleri with the evidence that had seemed so important to him.

And then, supposing Laurentano did find the courage to take action and some heedless colleague of his did manage to bring the case to trial, any lawyer could pick apart that evidence in the twinkling of an eye. But was it really because the evidence was negligible—it still was evidence, after all— that Spitaleri would not be found guilty? Or was it because in today's Italy, thanks to laws that increasingly favor the rights of the accused, what was lacking above all was a firm resolve to send anyone who committed a crime to prison?

But why, on the other hand, had the inspector had from the start, and continued to have, such a great desire to do harm to the developer? Because he was guilty of a building violation? Come on! If that was the case, then he should have something against half the population of Sicily, since the illegal constructions nearly outnumbered the legal ones.

Why had somebody died at one of his worksites?

And how many so-called accidents in the workplace were there that weren't accidents at all, but genuine homicides by the employers?

No, there was another reason.

It was Fazio's report that Spitaleri liked underage girls, and his own conclusion that the builder was a sex tourist to boot, that had made him develop a sort of violent aversion to the man. He couldn't stand the kind of people who took airplanes from one continent to another to go exploit poverty and material and moral misery in the most ignoble manner possible.

Someone like that, even if he lived in a palace in his home country, traveled first class, stayed in ten-star hotels, and ate in restaurants where a fried egg costs a hundred thousand euros, remained a wretch deep down in his soul, more wretched than the bastard who robs churches of their alms boxes or children of their lunch bags not because he's starving but for the sheer pleasure of doing so.

And men of that ilk are surely capable of the vilest, most loathsome sorts of acts.

At last, after some two hours, his eyelids started to droop. There was one finger of whisky left in the glass. He knocked it back and it went down the wrong way. As he was coughing, he remembered something Lozupone had said.

Which was that the autopsy had confirmed that the Arab had drunk too much, and had fallen for this reason.

But there was another possible hypothesis.

That the Arab, when he fell, had not died. He was only mortally wounded, and therefore able to swallow. And Spitaleri, Dipasquale, and Filiberto had taken advantage of the situation and forcibly plied him with wine. Then left him there to die alone.

They were capable of such an act, and the idea must have occurred to the one most capable of all, Spitaleri. And if things actually had happened the way he was imagining, it wasn't just he, Inspector Montalbano, who was being thwarted, but justice itself, indeed the very notion of justice.

He didn't sleep a wink all night. The rage in his body had redoubled the heat. He sweated so much that around four o'clock in the morning he got up and changed the bedsheets. But all for naught: Half an hour later they were as drenched as the ones he had just changed.

By eight o'clock he could no longer bear to stay in bed. Restlessness, nerves, and the heat were driving him crazy.

It occurred to him that Livia, on a boat out on the open sea, must be having a better time of it than he was. So he tried calling her on her cell phone. A recorded woman's voice informed him that the phone of the person he'd called was turned off and that, if he wished, he could try calling back later.

Naturally, at that hour the young lady was either sleeping or too busy helping her dear cousin Massimiliano to maneuver the boat! He suddenly felt itchy all over and started scratching himself until he bled.

Looking for a solution, he hopped down from the veranda and onto the beach. The sand was already hot and he risked burning the soles of his feet. He went for a long swim. Far from shore the water was still cool. But the refreshment didn't last long. In the time it took him to return to the house, he was already dry.

Why bother to go to the station? he asked himself.

He didn't have any pressing things to do; in fact, he didn't have anything at all to do. Tommaseo was busy with his press conference; Adriana had her sister's funeral to attend; the commissioner was probably too busy to look at the answers on the questionnaire he had sent to the different commissariats. And he, Montalbano, felt only like lolling about, but not at home.

"Catarella?"

"Atcher soivice, Chief."

"Lemme talk to Fazio."

"Straightaways."

"Fazio? I'm not coming in this morning."

"Don't feel well?"

"I feel just fine. But I'm convinced that I'll immediately feel bad if I come in to work."

"You're right, Chief. It's stifling here. Nobody can breathe."

"I'll come in this evening around six."

"Okay. Oh, Chief, could I borrow your minifan?"

"Be careful not to break it."

Half an hour later, on the road to Pizzo, he stopped in front of the rustic cottage, the one the peasant lived in. He got out of the car and approached the house. The front door was open. He called out.

"Anybody home?"

At the window directly above the door appeared the same man whose earthenware pot Gallo had shattered with the car. From the way the man looked at him, the inspector could tell he didn't recognize him.

"Whattya want?"

If he told him he was with the police, the guy might not let him in.

The homely clucking of some chickens behind the house came to his aid. He took a wild guess.

"Got any fresh eggs?"

"How many you need?"

It must not have been a big chicken coop.

"Half a dozen should do."

"Come on in."

Montalbano went in.

A bare room that must have served his every purpose. A table, two chairs, a cupboard. Against one wall, a small stove with a gas cylinder, and beside it a marble surface with glasses, dishes, a skillet, and a pot on top. Humble utensils worn out by time and overuse. Hanging on one wall was a hunting rifle.

The peasant came down the wooden stairs leading to the room above, which must have been his bedroom.

"I'll go get 'em for you."

He went outside. The inspector sat down in a chair.

The man returned with three eggs in each hand. He took two steps towards the small table, then stopped short. He stared hard at Montalbano as his face changed expression and paled.

"What's wrong?" the inspector asked him, getting up.

"Aaaaahhh!" the peasant roared.

And with all his might he hurled the three eggs in his right hand at Montalbano's head. Despite being caught by surprise, the inspector dodged two of them, whereas the third hit him on his left shoulder and broke, dripping down onto his shirt.

"Now I rec'nize ya, stinkin' cop!"

"But listen—"

"Still the same story? Eh?"

"No, I came to—"

Of the other three eggs, one got him on the forehead, and two in the chest.

Montalbano was blinded. He brought his handkerchief to his eyes to wipe them clean, and when he was able to see again through his gluey eyelids, he noticed that the peasant was now holding his hunting rifle and pointing it straight at him.

"Get out of my house, fuckin' cop!"

The inspector ran out.

His colleagues must have put the poor guy through a lot.

The stains had spread so far over his shirt that it looked one color in front and another in back.

He had to go back to Marinella to change clothes. There he found Adelina scrubbing the floor.

"Signò, what, somebuddy tro' eggs at you?"

"Yes, some poor bastard. I'm going to go change."

He washed himself with the hot water from the tanks on his roof, then put on a clean shirt.

"I'll be seeing you, Adelì."

"Signore, I gotta tell you I cannotta come tomorra."

"Why not?"

" 'Cause I'ma gonna go see my boy, the bigger one, who's in jail in Montelusa."

"How's the younger one doing?"

" 'E's in jail too, but in Palermo."

She had two sons, both delinquents, who were always in and out of jail.

Montalbano had sent them to jail a couple of times himself, but he still remained fond of them. He'd even been made godfather of one of them.

"Tell him I said hi."

"I will. I wannata say that since I'ma not coming, I make a you somethin a eat."

"Make me cold things, that way they'll last longer."

He headed back to Pizzo, bringing along his bathing suit this time.

He sped past the peasant's cottage, worried that the guy might shoot at his car, then past Adriana's house, the doors and windows of which were all shuttered, and pulled up at the illegal house.

Since he had the keys, he went inside, undressed, put on his bathing suit, went back outside, and descended the stone staircase to the beach. At this point there were few bathers, most of them speaking foreign languages. After August 15, Sicilians considered the summer season over, even if the heat was worse than before.

He retained a memory of clean, refreshing pleasure from the first time he had swum in those waters, when he came here with Callara. He dived into the sea and started swimming. He stayed in the water until the skin on his fingertips became wrinkled, a sign that it was time to return to shore.

His intention was to take a cold shower and go back home to eat whatever gift of God Adelina had prepared for him. But the climb up the staircase in the hot sun high overhead made him wilt, draining him of strength. Inside the house, he went straight into the master bedroom and lay down on the double bed.

It was two-thirty when he fell asleep and almost five when he woke up. The mattress bore the imprint of his naked body, a damp silhouette.

He stayed in the shower so long that he used up all the water in the tank. But since he wasn't at home, and since the house wasn't inhabited, he could do so without regrets.

When he went out to go to the station, he saw another car parked in front of the house. He thought he'd seen it before, but he couldn't remember where. There was nobody around. Maybe they'd gone down to the beach.

Then he noticed that an electrical cable had been plugged into the outlet next to the door and ran around the corner of the house to the back. Surely it was to illuminate the illegal apartment downstairs.

Who could it be? Certainly not anyone from Forensics. He was sure it must be some journalist who had come on the sly to take photos of the "site of the atrocious crime," and he felt suddenly overcome with rage.

How dared the brute?

He ran to his car, took his pistol out of the glove compartment, and slipped it inside his belt. Past the corner, the electrical cable continued along the wall, ran over the planks, and disappeared inside the window that served as an entrance to the illegal apartment.

He climbed lightly over the ledge and found himself in the bathroom. Cautiously craning his neck, he saw that the living room was illuminated.

That motherfucking photographer was surely hoping to get a scoop by taking pictures of the trunk in which the body had been found.

I'll give you a scoop, asshole, the inspector thought to himself.

And he did two things at once.

First, he set off running towards the living room, yelling: "Hands up!"

Second, he cocked his revolver and fired one shot in the air.

Now, either because the rooms were empty of furniture and amplified noise, or because the apartment was entirely covered in plastic, which didn't allow sound to disperse, the shot sounded like a huge explosion, barely less than a high-tonnage bomb blast.

The first person to take fright was Montalbano himself, who had the impression that the gun had exploded in his hand. Totally deafened by the blast, he burst into the living room.

In terror, the photographer had dropped his camera to the ground and, trembling all over, was kneeling down with his hands raised and his forehead on the ground. He looked like an Arab praying.

"You are under arrest!" the inspector said. "Montalbano's the name!"

"Wha—wha—" the man whimpered, barely raising his head.

"Why? You want to know why? Because you broke the seals to come inside!"

"But—but—there weren't ..."

"There weren't any seals!" said a quaking voice coming from it wasn't clear where. Montalbano looked around but didn't see anyone.

"Who said that?"

"I did."

And from behind the plastic-wrapped stack of casings Callara's head popped out.

"Inspector, you have to believe us: There weren't any seals!"

At that moment Montalbano remembered that when chasing after Adriana he hadn't had time to put them back.

"Must have been some young hoodlum who took them down," he said.

There in the living room the big floodlamp made the air even hotter than it would normally have been. One could barely speak, as the throat felt immediately parched.

"Let's get out of here," said the inspector.

They followed him into the apartment above, drank big glasses of mineral water, then sat down in the living room with the French doors wide open.

"I got so scared I nearly had a heart attack," said the man Montalbano had mistaken for a photographer.

"Me too," said Callara. "Every time I set foot in this damned house something strange happens to me!"

"My name's Paladino," the man with the camera introduced himself. "I'm a builder."

"But what were you guys doing here?"

Callara spoke first.

"You see, Inspector, since there's not much time left to make the amnesty requests, and since just this morning Signora Gudrun's papers arrived by courier, I pleaded with Mr. Paladino to start doing the things that need to be done—"

"And the first thing that absolutely needs to be done is to document and photograph the illegal construction," Paladino cut in. "The photos will then be attached to the blueprints."

"Did you finish photographing?"

"I need another three or four of the living room."

"Let's go."

He went out with them, accompanied them as far as the window, but did not go inside. Instead he stopped to collect the tape that had ended up under the two planks, and set them aside.

"I'll wait for you upstairs!"

He smoked two cigarettes while sitting on one end of the low wall along the terrace, in a spot where the sun wasn't beating down.

Then Callara came out.

"We're done."

"Where's Paladino?"

"Putting the equipment in the car. He'll be back in a second to say good-bye."

"If you need to come back here, let me know first."

"Thanks. By the way, I need to ask you something, Inspector."

"What?"

"When are the seals going to be taken down?"

"Are you in a hurry?"

"Well, sort of. I would like to set up a date with Spitaleri for digging the place out and restoring it. If I don't reserve in time, that guy, with all the things he's got going on . . ."

"If Spitaleri can't do it, just find someone else."

Paladino came back.

"We can go now."

"I can't look for anyone else," Callara said.

"What do you mean, you can't?"

"There's a pledge in writing that I didn't know about,

which I found among the papers that arrived this morning from Germany."

"Try to be a bit more specific."

"It's a standard agreement," said Paladino. "Callara showed it to me."

"What does it entail?"

This time it was Callara who spoke.

"It says that Angelo Speciale formally pledges to employ the firm of Michele Spitaleri to dig out and restore the outside and inside walls of the illegal apartment once amnesty is granted. And he also pledges not to turn to any other firms in the event that Spitaleri is busy with other jobs at the time, but to wait until he is available."

"A simple contract," said Montalbano.

"Yes, but properly executed, signed, and countersigned. And if one of the parties fails to uphold it, especially with a character like Spitaleri, they may have some big problems on their hands," said Paladino.

"Excuse me, Signor Paladino, but have you come across this sort of thing before?"

"This is the first time. I've never seen an agreement like this written so far in advance. And I don't quite understand it. I ask myself: What's a two-bit job like this to someone like Spitaleri?"

"I'm sure," said Callara, "it was Speciale who wanted this agreement. He knew he could count on Spitaleri, and that way there would be no need for him to be present at the moment the work got under way."

"Did you see the date?"

"Yes, October 27, 1999. The day before Angelo Speciale left to go back to Germany."

"Signor Callara, I'll see to having the seals removed as soon as possible."

In the meantime, he went and put the seals back up. Then he got in his car and left. But he braked after just a few yards.

The front door and two windows of Adriana's house were open. Had the girl perhaps gone there looking for a little serenity after the gloom of the funeral?

The inspector felt torn. Should he go see her or continue on his way?

Then he saw an elderly woman, a housekeeper, no doubt, close the two windows, one after the other. He waited a bit longer. The woman appeared in front of the door, then locked it.

Montalbano put the car in gear and headed back to the station, a little disappointed and a little relieved.

17

"This morning I went to the funeral," said Fazio.

"Were there a lot of people?"

"A lot, Inspector, all overcome with emotion, of course. Women fainting, women crying, former girlfriends from school with pale faces—the usual drama, in short. And when the coffin left the church, everyone started clapping. Can you tell me why anyone would clap for the dead?"

"Maybe because they thought she did the right thing by dying."

"Are you kidding, Chief?"

"No. When do people clap their hands? When they've seen something they like. Logically speaking, then, it should mean: I am rather pleased you are finally no longer in my hair. Who among the family members was there?"

"There was the father, who was being held up by a man and woman who must have been relatives of his. Miss Adriana wasn't there; she must have stayed home to help out her mother."

"I have to tell you something you're not going to like."

And he told him about his meeting with Lozupone. When he had finished, Fazio showed no surprise at all.

"You've got nothing to say?"

"What am I supposed to say, Chief? I was expecting it. By hook or by crook, Spitaleri's going to weasel his way out, now and forever, *in secula seculorum*."

"Amen. Speaking of Spitaleri, I want you to do me a favor and give him a call. I have no desire to speak with him."

"What do you want me to ask him?"

"If, that time he left for Bangkok on October the twelfth, he remembers what day he came back."

"I'll go do it right now."

He returned about ten minutes later.

"I tried him on his cell phone, but he had it turned off. So I called his office, but he wasn't in. The secretary, however, looked it up in an old agenda and said Spitaleri definitely returned on the afternoon of the twenty-sixth. She even told me she herself remembered the day very well."

"Did she say why?"

"Chief, that lady's such a chatterbox she's liable to go on talking all day if you don't stop her. She said October the twenty-sixth is her birthday, and she was thinking Spitaleri wouldn't remember, whereas Spitaleri brought her not only the orchid that Thai Airways gives to every passenger, but a box of chocolates. And there you have it. Why did you want to know?"

"Well, today I went to Pizzo to take a dip. As I was about to leave . . ."

And he told him the whole story.

"Which means," he concluded, "that the following day he drew up this personal contract, maybe because he'd found out that Angelo Speciale was about to leave for Germany."

"I don't see anything odd about it," said Fazio. "And I'm sure it was Speciale himself who asked for the contract, just as Callara says. By that point he trusted Spitaleri."

Montalbano seemed unconvinced.

"There's something that doesn't make sense to me."

The telephone rang. It was Catarella, terrified.

"Jesus Jesus Jesus! Iss the c'mishner onna line!"

"So?"

"He sounds crazy, Chief! Wit' all doo respeck, he sounds like a rapid dog!"

"Put him on and go have yourself a nip of cognac, it'll calm your nerves."

He turned on the speakerphone and gestured to Fazio to listen in.

"Good day, Mr. Commissioner."

"Good day, my ass!"

As far as he could remember, Montalbano had never heard Commissioner Bonetti-Alderighi use an obscenity. Whatever the problem was, it must have been big.

"Mr. Commissioner, I don't understand why—"

"The questionnaire!"

Montalbano felt relieved. Was that all? He gave a little smile.

"But Mr. Commissioner, the questionnaire in question is no longer in question."

Ah, what fun it was to apply every now and then the teachings of the great master Catarella!

"What are you saying?"

"I've already taken care of it and sent it over to you."

"Oh, you took care of it, all right! You really did take care of it!"

So why was he breaking their balls about it? What was the big deal? He translated these questions:

"So what's the problem?"

"Montalbano, are you working overtime at getting on my nerves today?"

That "working overtime" made the inspector stop joking and go on the counterattack.

"What the hell are you saying? You're raving, sir!"

The commissioner tried hard to calm down.

"Listen, Montalbano. I have the patience of Job, but if you're trying to make a fool of me ..."

Ah, "the patience of Job," too! Was the guy trying to drive him out of his mind?

"Just tell me what I did and stop threatening me."

"What you did? Why, you sent me last year's questionnaire, that's what you did! Did you get that? Last year's questionnaire!"

"My, how time flies!"

The commissioner was so beside himself that he didn't hear what the inspector said.

"I'm giving you two hours, Montalbano. I want you to find the new questionnaire, answer the questions, and fax it to me within two hours. Got that? Two hours!"

He hung up.

Montalbano looked disconsolately at the ocean of papers he would have to wade through again.

"Fazio, would you do me a favor?"

"At your service, Chief."

"Would you please shoot me?"

It took them three hours in all; two to find the questionnaire, one to fill it out. At a certain point they realized that it was exactly the same as the one from the previous year, with the same questions, in the same order; only the date in the heading had changed. They made no comments. By this point they no longer had the strength to say what they thought about bureaucracy.

"Catarella!"

"Here I am."

"Send this fax to the c'mishner right away and tell him to stick it you know where."

Catarella turned pale.

"I can't, Chief."

"That's an order, Cat!"

"Well, Chief, if you say it's an order . . ."

Resigned, he turned around to leave. But wait! Catarella was actually liable to do it!

"No, listen. Just send him the fax and don't say anything."

How many tons of dust can there be among the papers in an office? Back home, Montalbano stayed a good half an hour in the shower and then changed his clothes, which stank of sweat.

He was heading towards the refrigerator in his underpants to see what Adelina had prepared for him when the telephone rang.

It was Adriana. She didn't even say hi, didn't ask him how he was doing, but shot straight to the subject of interest to her.

"I can't make it to your place tonight. My nurse friend wasn't able to get free. She'll be coming here tomorrow morning. But you're working tomorrow morning, aren't you?"

"Yes."

"I want to see you."

Quiet, Montalbano, quiet. Bite your tongue, Salvo. Don't say "Me too," as you were about to do.

The girl's words, which were practically whispered, made him break into a sweat.

"I really, really want to see you."

The sweat on his skin started turning to steam, an ever so light, watery vapor, since it was still, at nine in the evening, hot enough to make one faint.

"You know what?" Adriana asked, changing tone.

"What?"

"Do you remember that uncle and aunt of mine who were supposed to leave to go back to Milan this afternoon?"

"Yes."

You couldn't say he wasted any words with Adriana.

"Well, they left the house, but when they got to the airport, they discovered that their flight had been canceled, along with all the others, because of a wildcat strike."

"So what did they do?"

"They decided to take the train, poor things. In this heat, you can imagine the kind of journey they'll have! Tell me what you were doing."

"Who, me?" he replied, taken by surprise by the sudden change in subject.

"Would Chief Inspector Salvo Montalbano like to say what he was doing at the moment he received a telephone call from the student, Miss Adriana Morreale?"

"I was on my way to the refrigerator to get something to eat."

"Where do you eat? In the kitchen, the way people who eat alone usually do?"

"I don't like eating in the kitchen."

"So where do you like to eat?"

"On the veranda."

"You have a veranda? That's fantastic! Do me a favor and set the table for two."

"Why?"

"Because I want to be there, too."

"But you just said you can't come!"

"No, silly, I meant in my mind. I want you to take a bite from my plate, and I'll take one from yours."

Montalbano's head started spinning slightly.

"O . . . okay."

"Bye. And good night. I'll phone tomorrow. I love you."

"Me t . . ."

"What did you say?"

"Meat. I said 'meat.' I was just thinking of what I was going to eat."

He'd saved himself by kicking the ball out of bounds.

"Oh, listen, I just had an idea. Why don't you call me down to the station for questioning tomorrow morning and grill me with one of those eye-to-eye investigations like Tommaseo wants to do?"

And she hung up laughing.

So much for the refrigerator! So much for eating! The only thing to do, and immediately, was to dive into the sea and go for a long swim, to cool his head and lower the temperature of his blood, which had now reached the boiling point. So now Adriana, too, was doing her best to increase the August heat?

As he was swimming in the dark of the night, a new torment began. It was a sensation he knew well. He turned over to float on his back, eyes open and gazing at the stars.

The sensation was one of a hand-drill beginning to bore into his brain. And it made the classic sound of a drill with each turn: *zzzrr . . . zzzrr . . . zzzrr . . .*

This tremendous nuisance—which no longer caused him any surprise, since it had been happening to him for years—meant that at some time during the preceding day he had heard something of great importance, something that might lead to a resolution of the case and to which he had not immediately paid any attention.

But when had he heard it? And who had said it?

Zzzrr . . . zzzrr . . . zzzrr . . .

Like a woodworm gnawing, making him nervous.

With broad, slow strokes, he returned to shore.

Entering his house, he realized his appetite was gone. So he grabbed a new bottle of whisky, a glass, and a pack of cigarettes and went and sat out on the veranda, dripping wet, without bothering to take off his bathing suit.

He racked his brains over and over, but nothing came back to him.

After an hour of this, he gave up. It used to be, he thought, that with a little concentration he could call to mind what was bothering him. *But when, exactly?* he asked himself. *When you were younger, Montalbà,* came the inevitable answer.

He decided to eat something. And he remembered that Adriana had asked him to set a place for her as well ... He was tempted to do so, but then felt ridiculous.

He set the table for only himself, went into the kitchen, put his hand on the refrigerator handle, still thinking of Adriana, and felt an electric shock.

How could that be? Apparently the refrigerator wasn't working properly. It was dangerous, in fact. He had to look into buying a new one.

But then, why, though his hand was still on the handle, did he feel no more shock? Want to bet that it wasn't an electrical shock at all, but something inside him, a short circuit in his head?

He'd felt the shock when he was thinking of Adriana! It was something the girl had said!

He went back out on the veranda. His appetite had disappeared again.

All at once Adriana's words resurfaced in his mind. He sprang to his feet, grabbed the cigarettes, and went walking along the water's edge.

Three hours later, he had finished the pack and his legs ached from the long walk. He went back home, looked at the clock. It was three in the morning. He washed, shaved, got all dressed up, then drank down a big mug of coffee. At a quarter to four he went out, got in his car, and drove off.

At that hour he could cruise in the cool of the night. At his customary pace, without needing to race around like Gallo.

He was chasing after a hope. One so subtle, so ethereal, that the slightest doubt would have made it disappear into thin air. Actually, to tell the truth, he was chasing after a wild idea.

When he pulled into Punta Raisi airport it was almost eight o'clock in the morning. It had taken him as long as it would have taken a normal driver to make a round trip. But it had been a peaceful ride. He hadn't felt hot and had had no occasion to grouse at any other drivers.

He parked and got out of the car. The air there was less oppressive than in Vigàta. One could actually breathe. The first thing he did was go to the bar: a double espresso, extra strong. Then he went to the airport police station.

"I'm Inspector Montalbano. Is Inspector Capuano here?"

Every time he went to the airport for Livia's arrival or departure, he would drop in on Capuano.

"He's just arrived. You can go in, if you like."

He knocked and entered.

"Montalbano! You waiting for your girlfriend?"

"No, I'm here to ask you to lend me a hand."

"I'm at your service. What is it?"

Montalbano told him.

"That'll take a little while. But I've got just the right person for it."

And he called out:

"Cammarota!"

He was a thirty-year-old, black as ink, eyes sparkling with intelligence.

"I want you to make yourself available to Inspector Montalbano, who's a friend of mine. You two can stay in here and use my computer. I have to go now and report to the commissioner."

They remained holed up in Capuano's office till noon, drinking two coffees and two beers each. Cammarota proved competent and clever, calling up a variety of ministries, airports, and airline companies. By the end, the inspector knew exactly what he had wanted to know.

When he got back in his car, he started sneezing, the delayed effect of the air-conditioning in Capuano's office.

Halfway home, he saw a trattoria with three tractor-trailers parked in front, a sure sign that the food was good. After ordering, he went to make a phone call.

"Adriana? Montalbano here."

"Oh, goody! Have you decided to give me the third degree?"

"I need to see you."

"When?"

"This evening around nine, at my house in Marinella. We'll have dinner there."

"I hope I can get organized in time. Is there any news?"

How did she know?

"I think so."

"I love you."

"Don't tell anyone you're going to my place."

"Are you kidding?"

Then he immediately called headquarters and asked for Fazio.

"Chief, where are you? I was looking for you this morning, because—"

"You can tell me later. I'm on my way back from Palermo and need to talk to you. We'll meet at the station at five. Be sure to drop all other engagements."

The restaurant had a great big ceiling fan that filled him with joy, allowing him to remain seated without having his shirt and underpants stick to his skin. As he'd expected, the food was good.

Getting back into the car, he thought that if, when he'd

left, his hope was thin as a spiderweb, now, on his return, it was thick as a rope.

A gallows rope.

He started singing, as off-key as a dog, *O Lola,* from *Cavalleria Rusticana.*

Back home in Marinella, he took a shower, changed clothes, and headed off in haste to the station. He felt sort of feverish and restless, irritated by the slightest thing.

"Aahhh, Chief, you gotta call from—"

"I don't give a shit who called. Send me Fazio right away."

He turned on the minifan. Fazio came running. The curiosity was eating him alive.

"Come in, close the door, and sit down."

Fazio obeyed and sat down at the edge of his chair, eyes trained on the inspector. He looked exactly like a hunting dog.

"Did you know there was a strike at Punta Raisi yesterday and most of the flights were canceled?"

"No, I didn't."

"I heard it on the regional news report."

It was a lie. He didn't want to tell him he'd heard it from Adriana.

"Okay, Chief, so there was a strike. Who doesn't go on strike these days? What's that got to do with us?"

"Oh, it's got a lot to do with us. A lot."

"I get it, Chief. You're beating around the bush just to make me stew a little."

"So? How many times have you done the same with me?"

"Fine, but now you've had your revenge. Talk."

"All right. So I heard about this strike but didn't pay any attention. Nevertheless, after a little while, an idea started to form in my head. I thought it over, and all at once, everything became clear to me. Crystal clear. So, very early this morning, I left for Punta Raisi. I had to see if my initial theory would check out."

"And did it?"

"Completely."

"So?"

"So, it means I know the name of Rina's killer."

"Spitaleri," Fazio said calmly.

18

"Oh, no you don't!" Montalbano raved. "You can't wreck my performance like that! It's not fair! I'm supposed to be the one to say the name! You have to show more respect for your superiors!"

"I won't say another word," Fazio promised.

Montalbano calmed down, but Fazio couldn't tell if he was seriously angry or only joking.

"How did you figure it out?"

"Chief, you went to Punta Raisi to confirm something. Until proven to the contrary, Punta Raisi is an airport. Now who, among the suspects, took an airplane? Spitaleri. Angelo Speciale and his stepson Ralf went by train. Correct?"

"Correct. So, when I heard the word 'strike,' it occurred to me that we had always taken for granted that Spitaleri's alibi was true. I had also learned that when our colleagues in Fiacca, who were handling the case of the disappearance, had pressed Spitaleri with questions, he had wiggled out with the story of his trip to Bangkok. And I thought they'd checked it out. Which is why we never asked him to give us proof that he actually left for Bangkok that day."

"But, Chief, we have indirect confirmation: Dipasquale and his secretary received a phone call from Spitaleri from a stopover along the way. And I'm convinced that phone call did take place."

"Yes, but who says it came from a stopover? If you call me long-distance direct from a public phone or cell phone, I don't know where you're calling from. You can say you're in Ambaradam or at the Arctic Circle, and I have no choice but to believe you."

"True."

"That's why I went to police headquarters at Punta Raisi. They were very nice. It took four hours, but I was right on target. That October twelfth was a Wednesday. The Thai Airways flight takes off from Fiumicino in Rome at two-fifteen P.M. Spitaleri leaves for Punta Raisi to catch a plane to Fiumicino that should get him there in time to catch the other flight. But, once at Punta Raisi, he finds out that the plane that's supposed to take him to Rome is delayed for two hours due to technical problems. Therefore he's not going to make it in time to catch the plane to Bangkok. So he's stranded at Punta Raisi. He manages to get his ticket changed to the next day. Not a big problem. The Thai flight for Thursday leaves Rome at two forty-five in the afternoon. Thus far, we're on safe ground."

"In what sense?"

"In the sense that we can document everything I've said. Now I'm going to make a conjecture. That Spitaleri, having nothing to do in Palermo, returns to Vigàta. I believe he took the Trapani road which, before getting here, passes by

Montereale. He decides then to see if the work at Pizzo has been finished. Bear in mind that the decision to wait till the following day to bury the illegal apartment was made by Dipasquale, and therefore Spitaleri doesn't know this. When he gets there, everybody's gone: the masons, Speciale, Ralf. He can see, however, that the illegal floor has not been covered up. One can still get inside. At this point—and this is my boldest conjecture—he happens to notice Rina in the vicinity. And it must have occurred to him that he himself, at that moment, in that place, did not exist."

"What do you mean, he didn't exist?"

"Think. There's no way Spitaleri can be at Pizzo at that time of the day. Everyone thinks he's on his way to Bangkok and, what's more, he hasn't yet returned to Vigàta. Therefore nobody knows he never left. What better opportunity? So he calls his office from his cell phone. That way he confirms his alibi. He thinks everything is all set, but he makes a big mistake."

"Namely?"

"The phone call itself. Apparently it had been at least three months since Spitaleri last went to Bangkok, because as of July, the Thai Airways flights from Rome became direct. There were no more stopovers."

"And what happened next, in your opinion?"

"Always remember I'm sailing on the seas of hypothesis. Thinking he's safe, he approaches Rina and, when he sees that the girl's not interested, he pulls out the knife he always carries with him—which he also pointed at Ralf, as Adriana told us—and forces her into the underground apartment. You can imagine the rest."

"No," said Fazio. "I don't want to imagine it."

"And this also explains the contract."

"The one with Speciale?"

"Exactly. The agreement he made with Speciale to fix up the house after amnesty was granted. There was one thing in it that seemed fishy to me, the bit about Speciale not being allowed to turn to any other business for the work. This meant Spitaleri wanted to be absolutely certain that he would be the one to dig out the illegal apartment, which would enable him to get rid of the trunk with the dead girl inside. This idea occurs to him while he's abroad, and that's why the moment he gets back, he races over to Speciale's, hoping he's still in Vigàta. Make sense to you?"

"Makes sense."

"So, in your opinion, what should I do now?"

"What do you mean, what should you do? Tomorrow morning you go to Prosecutor Tommaseo, you tell him the whole story and—"

"And I take it you know where."

"Why?"

"Because, since it involves somebody with connections like Spitaleri's, Tommaseo will proceed as if he's walking on eggshells. Not only. He'll find himself confronted by lawyers who'll eat him raw. Laying hands on Spitaleri means making life unpleasant for too many people: mafiosi, MP's, mayors. Everyone around him's on the take."

"Chief, Tommaseo may have a habit of losing his head around women, but when it comes to integrity—"

"But Tommaseo will be surrounded! If you like, I'll give you a little preview of Spitaleri's line of defense:

"'But on the morning of the twelfth, my client left Palermo on an earlier flight than the one that had the breakdown.'

"'But Spitaleri's name does not appear in any of the manifests of the earlier flights!'

"'Yes, but Rossi's does!'

"'And who is this Rossi?'

"'A passenger who gave up his seat, allowing Spitaleri to leave earlier to catch the flight to Bangkok.'"

"Can I do Tommaseo's part?" asked Fazio.

"Sure."

"'So how do you explain the telephone call from a stopover that never occurred?'"

After asking the question, he eyed the inspector with a look of triumph on his face. Montalbano laughed.

"You know how the lawyer will respond? Like this:

"'But my client called from Rome! The Thai flight that day took off at six-thirty P.M., not at two-fifteen!'"

"Is that really when it left?" asked Fazio.

"Yes. Except that Spitaleri didn't know there would be a delay. He thought the flight was already on its way to Bangkok."

Fazio twisted his face up in doubt.

"Of course, when you put it that way . . ."

"Don't you see I'm right? Our case risks ending up like the Arab mason's."

"So, what do think we should do?"

"We absolutely have to obtain a confession."

"Easy to say!"

"Look, there's no guarantee that we'll succeed in sending him to prison even with a confession. He'll say we tortured and beat him into confessing. A confession is the minimum we need just to take him to court."

"Okay, but how?"

"I've got a vague idea."

"Really?"

"Yes. But I don't want to talk about it here. Could we meet at my place tonight, around ten-thirty?"

It was eight o'clock when he got back to Marinella. The first thing he did was go out on the veranda.

There wasn't a breath of wind. The air felt like a heavy mantle that had been cast over the earth. The heat absorbed by the sand during the day was only now beginning to rise in a vapor, making the atmosphere feel hotter and more humid. The sea seemed dead, the white foam of the surf a kind of drool.

His agitation over Adriana's visit and the things he would have to ask her made him sweat as if he were in a sauna.

He took off his clothes and went to the refrigerator in only his underpants. He was dumbstruck. He remembered that he hadn't looked inside the fridge since Adelina told him she was going to make him enough food for two days.

What he was looking at wasn't the inside of a refrigerator, but a corner of La Vucciria, the great Palermo market. He inhaled the scent of dish after dish, and it was all still fresh.

He set the table on the veranda. He brought out green olives, cured black *passuluna* olives, celery, caciocavallo cheese, and six dishes, one with fresh anchovies, one with *calamaretti,* another with *purpiteddri,* another with squid, another with tuna, and another with sea snails. Each was dressed in a different manner, and there were still other things to eat in the fridge.

Afterwards he took a shower, changed his clothes, and decided to call Livia. He needed to hear her voice at the very least. Perhaps to steel himself for Adriana's imminent visit? He was greeted by the same recording of a woman's voice telling him that the telephone of the person he'd called was either turned off or unreachable.

Unreachable! What the hell was that supposed to mean?

But why was Livia making herself unavailable at the very moment he needed her most? Was it possible she couldn't hear the silent SOS he was sending her? Was the young lady perhaps too distracted by the diversions, indeed the entertainments, being provided by cousin Massimiliano?

As he grew more and more furious, not knowing whether the cause was a bout of jealousy or wounded pride, the doorbell rang. He was unable to move. A second ring, longer this time.

He finally went to open the door, walking like a combination of a condemned man on his way to the electric chair and a fifteen-year-old on his first date, already drenched in sweat.

Adriana, wearing jeans and a blouse, kissed him lightly on the lips, as if they'd long been intimate, and entered the house, brushing against him.

How could it be that in this terrible heat the girl always smelled so cool and fresh?

"It took some doing," she said, "but I finally made it here! Would you believe I feel sort of moved? Let me see."

"See what?"

"Your house."

She had a careful look around, room after room, as if she was going to buy it.

"What side do you sleep on?" she asked, standing at the foot of the bed.

"Over there. Why?"

"No reason. Just curious. What's your girlfriend's name?"

"Livia."

"Where's she from?"

"Genoa."

"Let me see the picture."

"Of what?"

"Your girlfriend, what else?"

"I haven't got one."

"Come on, I won't eat it."

"It's true, I haven't got any."

"Why not?"

"Dunno."

"Where's she now?"

"She's unreachable."

It had slipped out. Adriana gave him a confused look.

"She's on a boat with other friends," he explained.

Why hadn't he told her the truth?

"Everything's ready on the veranda, come," he said, to steer her away from that delicate subject.

Seeing the table set, Adriana balked.

"It's true I like to eat, but all this stuff . . . God, it's so beautiful here!"

"You sit down first."

Adriana sat down on the bench but slid over only a little, so that in order for Montalbano to sit down, he practically had to press against her.

"I don't like this," said Adriana.

"You don't like what?"

"Sitting this way."

"You're right, it's too tight. If you would just slide over a little . . ."

"That's not what I meant. I don't like eating without looking at you."

Montalbano went to get a chair and sat down in front of her.

He, too, felt better with a little distance between them.

But how was it that, even as the night progressed, the heat remained so intense?

"Could I have a little wine?"

He took out a strong, chilled white. It went down the throat like a dream. There were two more bottles of it in the fridge.

"Before I begin, I have to ask you something I'm anxious to know."

"I haven't got a boyfriend. And right at this moment I'm not with anyone."

The inspector felt embarrassed.

"That's not what ... I didn't mean ... Do you know Spitaleri personally?"

"The builder? The one who saved Rina from Ralf? No, we were never introduced."

"How come? After all, you and your sister lived just a few yards away from his worksite."

"True. But, you see, during that period I was living more with my aunt and uncle in Montelusa than with my parents in Pizzo. I never met him."

"Are you sure?"

"Yes."

"What about afterwards? During the search for Rina?"

"My aunt and uncle took me back to Montelusa almost immediately. My parents were too involved with the search, they couldn't sleep, couldn't eat. My aunt and uncle wanted to take me away from that stressful atmosphere."

"More recently?"

"I don't think so. I didn't go to the funeral, I stayed away from the television interviews. Only one newspaper wrote that Rina had a sister, but they didn't specify that we were twins."

"Shall we start eating?"

"Gladly. Why did you ask me about Spitaleri?"

"I'll tell you later."

"You'd said earlier there was some news."

"We'll talk about that later, too."

———

They were eating in silence, occasionally looking each other in the eye, when all of a sudden Montalbano felt one of Adriana's knees press against his. He spread his legs slightly, and the girl's leg slid between them. Then, with her other leg, Adriana took one of his prisoner, squeezing it hard.

It was a miracle the inspector kept the wine from going down the wrong way. But he felt his face blushing red and got angry with himself.

Later, Adriana gestured towards the sea snails.

"How is one supposed to eat those?"

"You have to pull them out with a big sort of hairpin that I put among the silverware at your place."

Adriana tried opening one but didn't succeed.

"You do it for me," she said.

Montalbano used the pin, and she opened her mouth and let him feed her.

"Mmm. It's good. More."

Each time she opened her mouth for the snail, Montalbano nearly had a heart attack.

The bottle of wine was emptied in a flash.

"I'll go open another."

"No," said Adriana, squeezing his imprisoned leg, but she must have immediately noticed his anxiety. "Okay," she said, liberating him.

Returning with the opened bottle, the inspector didn't sit back down in the chair, but on the bench, beside Adriana.

When they had finished eating, Montalbano cleared the table, leaving the bottle and glasses. As he sat back down, Adriana tucked herself under his arm and leaned her head on his shoulder.

"Why do you keep running away?"

Had the moment come to talk seriously? Perhaps that was best, to confront the question head-on.

"Adriana, believe me, I have no desire whatsoever to run away from you. I like you in a way that has rarely happened to me. But do you realize that there's a thirty-three-year age difference between us?"

"I'm not asking you to marry me."

"Okay, but it's the same thing. I'm practically an antique, and it really doesn't seem right to me that ... Someone the right age, on the other hand ..."

"But what's the right age, anyway? Twenty-five? Thirty? Have you seen the men that age? Have you heard them speak? Do you know how they act? They have no idea what women are about!"

"Listen, to you I'm just a passing desire, but for me, you risk becoming something else entirely. At my age—"

"Enough of this age stuff. And don't imagine I want you the way I might want an ice cream cone. Speaking of which, have you got any?"

"Ice cream? Yes."

He took it out of the freezer, but it was so hard he was unable to cut into it. He brought it out on the veranda.

"Custard and chocolate. Sound okay to you?" asked Montalbano, sitting back down as before.

And, as before, she tucked herself under his arm and leaned her head on his shoulder.

Five minutes were enough to make the ice cream edible. Adriana ate hers in silence, without changing position.

Then, as Montalbano was pushing away her empty plate, he realized the girl was crying. The sound of it wrung his heart. He tried to make her raise her head from his shoulder so he could look her in the eye, but she resisted.

"There's another thing you have to consider, Adriana. That for years I've been with a woman I love. And I've always tried as best I can to remain faithful to Livia, who is—"

"Unreachable," said Adriana, raising her head and looking him in the eye.

The same thing must have happened to men in castles under siege during the wars of yesteryear. They would hold out a long time against hunger and thirst, pour boiling oil to repel those climbing the walls, and the castle would seem impregnable. And then a single shot of the catapult, precise and well-aimed, would knock down the iron door, and the besiegers would burst in, encountering no more resistance.

Unreachable. That was the key word Adriana had used. What had the girl heard in that word when he'd used it? His anger? His jealousy? His weakness? His loneliness?

Montalbano embraced her and kissed her. Her lips tasted of custard and chocolate.

It was like plunging into the great August heat.

Then Adriana said:

"Let's go inside."

They stood up, still embracing, and at that moment the doorbell rang.

"Who could that be?" asked Adriana.

"It's ... it's Fazio. I told him to come. I'd forgotten all about it."

Without a word, Adriana went and locked herself in the bathroom.

As soon as he set foot on the veranda, Fazio, seeing the two glasses and the two small dishes streaked with ice cream, asked:

"Is there another person here?"

"Yes, Adriana."

"Ah. And is she leaving now?"

"No."

"Ah."

"Like a glass of wine?"

"No, sir, thanks."

"A bit of ice cream?"

"No, sir, thanks."

Clearly he felt irritated by the girl's presence.

19

They'd been sitting on the veranda for nearly an hour, but even as the night advanced, it brought no relief. In fact, the heat seemed more rabid than ever, as if there wasn't a half-moon in the sky but the midday sun.

When he'd finished talking, he looked inquisitively at Fazio.

"What do you think?" he said.

"So you would like to call Spitaleri in to the station for questioning, subject him to one of those interrogations that last a day and a night, and then, when he's reduced to the state of a doormat, have Miss Adriana, who he's never seen before, suddenly appear before him. Is that what you're saying?"

"More or less."

"And you think that when he sees the twin sister of the girl he killed standing in front of him, he'll crack and confess?"

"At least I'm hoping that's what he'll do."

Fazio twisted up his mouth.

"Not convinced?"

"Chief, the guy's a crook. He's got thicker skin than an armadillo. The moment you call him in for questioning, he's gonna go on the defensive and put on his armor, because he'll expect the works from you. So even if he sees the girl and has a heart attack, I'm sure he won't let it show."

"So you think it's useless to have Adriana appear by surprise?"

"No, I think it could be useful, but I think it would be a mistake to have it take place at the police station."

Adriana, who'd been silent up until then, finally spoke.

"I agree with Fazio. It's not the right setting."

"What would be the right one, in your opinion?"

"The other day I suddenly realized that after amnesty is granted, other people will move into that house and live there. And it didn't seem right to me. The idea that others might, I dunno, laugh and sing . . . in the same living room where Rina had her throat slashed . . ."

She made a sort of sobbing sound. Instinctively Montalbano put his hand on hers. Fazio noticed, but showed no surprise. Adriana pulled herself together.

"I've decided to talk about it with Papa."

"What do you want to do?"

"I want to suggest that he should sell our house and buy the one in which Rina died. That way the illegal apartment will never be lived in by anyone, and my sister's memory will remain free."

"And what do you expect to achieve by this?"

"You just mentioned the exclusive contract Spitaleri has for refurbishing the house. Well, tomorrow morning, I'm going to that agency and I'm going to tell that man, what's his name . . ."

"Callara."

"I'm going to tell Callara we want to buy the house, even before amnesty is granted. We'll take care of all the paperwork and cover all the expenses for the amnesty. I'll explain to him why, and let him know that we're willing to pay well for it. I'll convince him, I'm sure of it. Then I'll ask him to give me keys to the upstairs apartment and to recommend somebody to handle the renovation of the downstairs. At which point Callara will surely give me Spitaleri's name. I'll get the phone number, and then—"

"Wait a minute. What if Callara wants to come along with you?"

"He won't if I don't tell him exactly when I'm going to go. He can't remain at my disposal for two whole days. Anyway, I think the fact that we own a house just a few yards away from his will work in my favor."

"And then what?"

"Then I'll phone Spitaleri and have him come out to Pizzo. If I can manage to be downstairs, in the living room where he murdered Rina, at the moment he arrives, and he sees me there for the first time—"

"You can't be left alone with Spitaleri!"

"I won't be alone, if you're there hiding behind that stack of window frames."

"How do you know there are frames in the living room?" asked an alert Fazio, like the smart cop he always was, even in friendly surroundings.

"I told her myself," Montalbano cut in.

Silence fell over the three of them.

"If we take all the necessary precautions," the inspector said a moment later, "maybe we could pull it off."

"Chief, can I speak freely?" Fazio asked.

"Of course."

"With all due respect to the young lady, I don't like the idea."

"Why not?" asked Adriana.

"It's extremely dangerous, Miss. Spitaleri always goes around with a knife in his pocket, and the man is capable of anything."

"But if Salvo is also there, it seems to me—"

Fazio didn't show any surprise at that "Salvo," either.

"I still don't like it. It's not right for us to put you in danger that way."

They discussed things for another half hour. In the end, it was Montalbano who decided.

"We're going to do what Adriana suggested. For additional security, you'll be in the vicinity, too, Fazio, perhaps with another one of our men."

"Whatever you say, sir," said Fazio, surrendering.

He stood up, said good-bye to Adriana, and headed towards the door, with the inspector following behind him. But before leaving, he looked Montalbano in the eye.

"Chief, think long and hard about it, before you give the final go-ahead."

"Come and sit down," Adriana said when Montalbano returned.

"I'm a little tired," he said.

Something had changed, and the girl realized it.

In his lonely bed, between sweat-dampened sheets, Montalbano had a wretched night, feeling one minute like an utter fool, the next minute like San Luigi Gonzaga or Sant'Alfonso de' Liguori, somebody like that.

Adriana's first phone call to Montalbano came into the station around five o'clock in the afternoon the following day.

"I got the keys from Callara. He's thrilled about selling right away. He must be rather greedy, because when he heard that we would absorb all the costs of the amnesty, he practically got down on his knees in thanks."

"Did he tell you about Spitaleri?"

"He even showed me the contract he made with Speciale, and gave me Spitaleri's cell phone number into the bargain."

"Have you called him?"

"Yes. I spoke directly with him. We made an appointment to meet at the house tomorrow evening at seven. So, where do we stand with our plans?"

"We'll meet at the house tomorrow around five P.M. That should give us enough time to organize everything well."

Her second call, on the other hand, was to Marinella, around ten o'clock that evening.

"The nurse just arrived. She's going to spend the night. Can I come see you?"

What did it mean? Did she want to spend the night with him?

Was she joking? He couldn't handle another night playing the part of Saint Anthony being tempted by demons in the desert.

"Look, Adriana, I—"

"I feel extremely nervous and need some company."

"I understand perfectly. I'm nervous, too."

"I'll just come for a nighttime swim. Come on."

"Why don't you just go to bed? Tomorrow will be a hard day."

She giggled.

"No problem, I'll bring my bathing suit."

"Oh, all right."

Why had he given in? Weariness? Because of the heat, which killed the will? Or simply because he himself, really and truly, felt like seeing her?

The girl swam like a dolphin. And Montalbano experienced a new, troubling pleasure, feeling that young body beside his, making the same movements as if long accustomed to swimming with him.

Adriana, moreover, had so much stamina, she could have swum all the way to Malta. At a certain point, Montalbano couldn't go any farther and flipped over to do the dead man's float. She came back and floated right beside him.

"Where did you learn how to swim?"

"I took a lot of lessons when I was little. When I come here in the summer I spend the whole day in the water. In Palermo I go to the pool twice a week."

"Do you do a lot of sports?"

"I go often to the gym. I can even shoot a gun."

"Really?"

"Yes. I used to have a . . . well, let's call him a boyfriend, who was a fanatic. He used to take me to the Poligono."

A pang, ever so slight. Not of jealousy, but of envy for the boy, her former . . . well, let's call him her lover, who was the right age and could enjoy her company without complications.

"Shall we go back?" said Adriana.

They took their time swimming back. Neither of them wanted to break the sort of spell that had fallen over their bodies, which they couldn't see in the darkness but could therefore feel all the more through their breath and the occasional moments of contact.

Then, about two or three yards from the shore, where the water was waist-deep, Adriana, who was holding Montalbano's hand as she walked, slammed her foot against a metal jerry can that some asshole had thrown into the water, and fell forward. Instinctively, Montalbano gripped her hand, but then, perhaps because he lost his balance, he fell in turn, right on top of the girl.

They resurfaced in each other's clutches as though wrestling, and breathless as if after a long submersion. Adriana slipped again, and they both collapsed underwater, still in each other's arms. They emerged even more tightly embraced, and then drowned themselves once and for all in other waters.

When, much later, Adriana finally left, another nasty night began for Montalbano, who spent it thrashing back and forth, tossing and turning and burning up.

The heat, naturally. And a feeling of guilt, of course. Perhaps even a sense of shame. A hint of self-loathing as well. And throw in a pinch of remorse.

Above all, however, a deep melancholy over a question that had treacherously caught him off-guard: *If you hadn't been fifty-five years old, would you have been able to say no? Not to Adriana, but to yourself? And the answer could only be: Yes, I would have been able to say no. After all, I'd done so before.*

So then why did you give in to a part of yourself that you've always been able to keep in line?

Because I'm not as strong as before. And I knew it.

So it was the very awareness of your approaching old age that made you weak in front of Adriana's youth and beauty?

And this time, too, the bitter answer was yes.

"Chief, wha'ss wrong?"

"Why?"

"Y'oughta see your face! You feel sick?"

"I didn't sleep, Cat. Get me Fazio."

Fazio's face didn't look too pretty either.

"Chief, I didn't sleep a wink all night. Are you sure about what we're doing?"

"I'm not sure about anything. But it's the only way."

Fazio threw up his hands.

"Post a guard at the house starting now. I wouldn't want some idiot entering the illegal apartment and screwing everything up. Then have him go off at five, since by that time we'll be there. Also, get your hands on a twenty-yard extension cord with a three-outlet adapter, and buy three mechanic's lamps from the repair shop. You know, the kind that have a protective grating for the bulb?"

"Yessir. But what's all this material for?"

"We'll hook into the power from the outlet next to the front door and bring it down into the illegal apartment, the way Callara did when he brought that builder there. We'll plug the three mechanic's lamps into the adapter, two of which will go in the living room. At least there'll be some light."

"But won't all this getup make Spitaleri suspicious?"

"Adriana can always tell him it was Callara who suggested it. Who you going to bring along?"

"Galluzzo."

He was unable to do anything. He took no calls, signed no papers. He kept his head close to the minifan. At moments, images of himself and Adriana from the night before came into his mind, and he immediately blotted them out. He wanted to concentrate on what might happen with Spitaleri, but there was no way. Above all else, the sun that day would have roasted a lizard. It was like when, towards the end of a fireworks display, the most colorful rockets burst in the sky and the most powerful booms explode; in the same way, August, during its final phase, was firing its most torrid, scorching days at them. After he didn't know how long, Fazio came in and told him he had got all the material.

"It's murder out there, Chief."

They reconfirmed the plan to meet at the house at five.

The inspector didn't feel like leaving the office to go eat. He didn't even feel hungry.

"Catarella, don't put any calls through and don't let anyone into my office."

Like the other time, he locked his door, took off his clothes, pointed the minifan at the armchair, which he had pulled up to the desk, and sat down in his underpants. A little while later he nodded off.

When he woke up it was four o'clock. He went into the bathroom, stripped down naked, washed himself with water so warm it felt like piss, put his clothes back on, went out, got in his car, and headed for Pizzo.

Adriana's and Fazio's cars were parked in front of the house. Before getting out, he opened the glove compartment, took out his pistol, and slipped it into the back pocket of his trousers.

They were all in the living room. Adriana smiled and shook hands with him. This time her hand was ice-cold, a relief.

Was the formality for Galluzzo's benefit?

"Fazio, did you bring the equipment?"

"Yessir."

"Hook up the lights at once."

Fazio and Galluzzo left. They were barely out the door when Adriana came over and hugged Montalbano.

"I love you even more today."

And she kissed him. He managed to resist, gently pushing her away.

"Adriana, try to understand. I have to be lucid."

Slightly disappointed, the girl went out on the terrace. He rushed into the kitchen. Luckily there was a bottle of cold water in the refrigerator. To avoid complications, he didn't move from that spot. A few minutes later, he heard Galluzzo calling him.

"Chief, want to come and have a look?"

He went out on the terrace.

"Come with me," he said to Adriana.

Fazio had placed a lamp just outside the small bathroom and the other two in the living room. The light barely sufficed to let one see where one was stepping, whereas people's faces were like frightening masks: the eyes disappeared, the mouths were black holes, the shadows on the walls loomed large and menacing. Just as on the set of a horror film. It was stifling down there, one could barely breathe. It was like being in a submarine that had long been underwater.

"Okay," said Montalbano. "Let's go."

Once outside, he said:

"Let's get those cars out of here immediately. Only the young lady's car should be in front of the house. Adriana, give me the keys to your house."

He took them and gave them to Fazio. Then he pulled out the keys to his car and handed them to Galluzzo.

"You take mine. Park them behind Adriana's house so they can't be seen from the road. Then go inside and watch for Spitaleri's car from two different windows. As soon as you see it, you, Fazio, will warn me with one ring on my cell phone and come running. Is that clear? By the time Spitaleri goes downstairs, both of you should already be here and positioned in such a way that, no matter what happens, he can't escape. Is that clear?"

"Perfectly," said Fazio.

They sat on the sofa in each other's arms and didn't say a word.

Not because they had nothing to say to one another, but because they felt that it was better this way. At a certain point the inspector looked at his watch.

"Just ten minutes more. Maybe we'd better go downstairs."

Adriana grabbed the bag with the documents to the house and slung it across her chest.

When they were in the living room, Montalbano immediately tried hiding behind the stack of frames. There wasn't much room; they were too close to the wall. Sweating and cursing, he pushed them forward, making them lean a bit. He tried again and felt more comfortable; he could move without hindrance.

"Can you see me?" he asked Adriana.

No answer. He stuck his head out and saw the girl teetering in the middle of the room like a tree in the wind. He realized that, at the last minute, Adriana had been seized by a fit of panic. He ran to her and she embraced him, trembling.

"I'm so afraid, so afraid."

She seemed very upset. Montalbano was calling himself a fool and an idiot. He hadn't thought of the effect that being in that place would have on the girl's nerves.

"Let's drop everything and leave."

"No," she said, "wait."

She was making an enormous effort to control herself, and it showed.

"Give me . . . give me your gun."

"Why?"

"Let me hold it. It'll make me feel safer. I'll put it in my purse."

Montalbano pulled out the weapon, but didn't hand it over. He was undecided.

"Adriana, you have to realize that—"

At that moment they heard Spitaleri's voice nearby:

"Signorina Morreale? Are you here?"

He must have been calling from the window of the small bathroom. Why hadn't the inspector's cell phone worked?

Were they out of range down there? With one swift motion Adriana took the gun from his hand and put it in her purse.

"I'm here, Signor Spitaleri," she said, suddenly calm, her voice sounding almost cheerful.

Montalbano barely had time to hide.

He heard Spitaleri's steps as he entered the living room. And again Adriana's voice, this time transformed, silvery, like that of the adolescent she'd once been.

"Come, Michele."

How did she know Spitaleri's first name? Had she read it in the documents Callara had given her? And why such familiarity?

Then there was silence. What was happening? And, suddenly, a laugh, but all broken apart, like pieces of glass falling to the floor. Was it Adriana who was laughing that way? Then, finally, Spitaleri's voice.

"You . . . you're not . . . ?"

"Want to try again with me? Hmm? Go ahead and try, Michele. Look. How do you like me?"

Montalbano heard a sound of ripping fabric. *Matre santa*, what was Adriana doing? Then Spitaleri bellowed:

"I'll kill you too! Slut! You're an even bigger whore than your sister!"

Montalbano leapt out. Adriana had torn open her blouse, her tits hanging out. Spitaleri, knife in hand, was advancing towards her. He was walking stiffly, like a mechanical puppet.

"Stop!" the inspector shouted.

But Spitaleri didn't even hear him. He took another step,

and Adriana fired. A single shot. Straight to the heart, as she'd practiced at the Poligono. As Spitaleri fell onto the trunk, Montalbano ran up to Adriana and grabbed the pistol from her hand. Face to face, they eyed one another. And, feeling the ground give way under his feet, the inspector understood.

Fazio and Galluzzo came running in, weapons in hand, and froze.

"He tried the same thing with her," said Montalbano as Adriana was trying to cover up her breasts with her torn blouse. "So I was forced to shoot him. Look, he's still holding the knife."

Throwing the gun to the floor, he left the room and, once outside the illegal apartment, started running as if being chased. He raced down the stone staircase, two steps at a time, to the beach, where, all at once, he tore off all his clothes, not giving a damn about the couple staring at him in shock, and dived into the sea.

He swam and he wept. Out of anger, humiliation, shame, disappointment, wounded pride.

For not having realized that Adriana was using him to achieve her end, which was to kill with her own hands the man who had slashed her sister's throat.

With the phony "I love you," the phony passion, the phony fear, she had led him step by step where she wanted to go. He had been a puppet in her hands.

All theater. All make-believe.

While he, dazzled by beauty and lost in pursuit of intoxi-cating youth, had fallen for it, at fifty-five years of age and more, like a child.

He swam and he wept.

NOTES

2 her Joyful and not-so-Joyful Mysteries: The Joyful Mysteries represent five of the traditional fifteen Mysteries of the Rosary, the other ten being the five Sorrowful Mysteries and the five Glorious Mysteries. In 2002 Pope John Paul II added five new "optional" Mysteries, the Luminous Mysteries. The Joyful Mysteries concern the early episodes in the life of Christ and the Virgin Mary, namely the Annunciation, the Visitation, the Nativity, the Presentation of Jesus in the Temple, and the Finding of Jesus in the Temple.

31 "I don't want the media finding out. I don't want another Vermicino": Montalbano is alluding to the harrowing three-day ordeal of Alfredino Rampi, a six-year-old boy who fell into an artesian well only 30 centimeters (about 1 foot) wide and 80 meters (about 90 yards) deep in the township of Vermicino near Rome in June of 1981. The event was covered nonstop for eighteen hours by the three national RAI television stations and ended in tragedy. After two failed rescue attempts, in which the boy fell farther down into the well, Alfredino was found dead upon the third attempt, probably from injuries sustained in his repeated falls.

39 "this government has granted one amnesty after another": The fire chief is alluding to certain policies of the government of media tycoon Silvio Berlusconi, which granted amnesty on a variety of fiscal and other violations, including those of tax dodgers who had parked vast sums of money in financial havens abroad and those of builders who had ravaged much of the landscape, especially in the south, with illegal constructions in violation of zoning codes.

83 "Don't you pay for protection?": That is, Mafia "protection." In the original, Camilleri uses the word *pizzo* (which literally means "point" or "tip"), the Sicilian term used for the payoff required of businesses operating on Mafia turf. There is perhaps a bit of irony in the author's also calling the district in which the illegally built house is situated "Pizzo," which in this case refers no doubt to the promontory or "point" on which it stands.

104 "the period of cooperation between all the different commissariats regardless of regional boundaries": In the Italian police bureaucracy the administrative term for a police department the size of that under Montalbano's direct authority is *commissariato,* and the various *commissariati* fall under the authority of the *questura,* here represented by the commissioner's office in Montelusa. Normally the chain of command and jurisdiction is determined territorially, but during the period alluded to by Fazio, the *commissariati* of different jurisdictions were supposed to "cooperate," leading, Italian-style, to a great deal of confusion.

111 Ah, servile Italy ... a brothel!: *Purgatorio* 6:77–79; my translation.

111 Italy was still servile ... thanks to a helmsman whom she would be better off without: The "helmsman" being, of course, Silvio Berlusconi.

114 *Lupus in fabula:* Latin, literally, "a wolf in the story." The figurative meaning is the same as "speak of the devil."

122 "But tomorrow is August the fifteenth!": August 15 is *Ferragosto*, the biggest holiday of the summer.

133 "Better sunstroke than looking like somebody going to the Pontida meetings": Montalbano is referring to the politicians of the secessionist extreme-right Lega Nord (Northern League), who stage their political summits at Pontida in northern Italy and are fond of wearing baseball caps.

133 *"Vocumprà?":* A common refrain recited by foreign street peddlers in Italy, usually of North African or sub-Saharan origin. The word is a corruption of the phrases *Vuoi comprare* or *Vuole comprare,* both of which mean, "Do you want to buy?"

168 a quatrain by Pessoa: Fernando Pessoa (1888–1935) was Portugal's greatest modern poet.

190 he was acting like the soldier who doesn't want to go to war: A reference to the Sicilian expression *fari u fissu pri nun iri a la guerra,* which means to feign ignorance to avoid doing something unpleasant. Literally, the phrase means "to play dumb so as not to go to war."

207 "Maybe we ought to use little folded-up pieces of paper, like Provenzano": Montalbano is referring to the famous *pizzini* of Bernardo Provenzano, the Mafia "boss of bosses" arrested in 2006 after forty-three years on the run. Provenzano used these little folded-up messages to communicate his orders to the various agents of his crime network. In an April 21, 2006, op-ed in the *New York Times,* written on the occasion of Provenzano's arrest, Camilleri stated: "The authorities said that Mr. Provenzano would transmit his orders—regarding such matters as who should be rewarded with government contracts, whom one should vote for in local and national elections, how one should act on specific occasions—by means of *pizzini,* little scraps of paper folded several times over, which his trusty couriers (mostly peasants with spotless records) would pass from hand to hand along lengthy, circuitous, and seemingly random routes. These were necessary precautions to reduce, as much as possible, the risk of interception. One *pizzino,* for example, took more than forty-eight hours to travel the mile between the boss's cottage and Corleone. Others could take weeks to reach a nearby destination. The telephone was out of the question. In every *pizzino,* there was always a mention of God and his will and protection."

In 2007 Camilleri published a book on Provenzano's *pizzini* entitled *Voi non sapete* (You Don't Know) in which he explains, in the form of a dictionary, some sixty of the Sicilian words most frequently used by the crime boss. The book's title refers to Provenzano's statement to the authorities upon arrest, in which he was alluding to the Mafia war that he thought would break out after his removal from power. All proceeds from the book go to a charitable organization founded to help victims of Mafia violence.

Notes by Stephen Sartarelli

AVAILABLE FROM PENGUIN

The Inspector Montalbano Series

**PENGUIN
BOOKS**